The Atlantis Gene

Book 3

The Atlantis Saga

S.A. Beck

ISBN-13: 978-1987859300
ISBN-10: 1987859308

Contents

Chapter 1

JUNE 12, 2016, MOJAVE DESERT, NEVADA

11:45 AM

Even though it was barely past noon, Otto Heike felt exhausted. He slumped in the back of the Subaru and watched the desert go by. He'd had a sleepless night during an eleven-hour drive in that very same car, a terrifying morning making contact with a scientist who should have been lying half dead in a hospital bed, and then a tense hour driving out of Albuquerque, wondering when they were going to get shot.

The shots never came, and fatigue was getting the better of his fear. His eyes kept closing, and his thoughts became muddled. Then an awareness of their situation jerked him awake, and he looked behind them on the lonely desert road, searching for pursuit.

Next to him sat the scientist they had gone to Albuquerque to pick up, Dr. Akiko Yamazaki, a middle-aged woman who his friends in the Atlantis Allegiance had told him had suffered a massive stroke. She seemed fine at the moment, though, and had told them a story about how a group of Atlanteans had come into her hospital room, magically healed her by laying their hands on her head, and whisked her away as they were chased by cops and government agents who killed all the Atlanteans while Dr. Yamazaki made her escape.

That last part sounded magical too.

Otto was having a hard time buying her story. There were too many unbeliev-able things about it. But if someone was going to make up a bogus story, would they make up one that made no sense? Dr. Yamazaki seemed too intelligent to devise such a lousy alibi.

His companions in the front seat looked as confused as he was.

Dr. James Yuhle was driving and kept glancing at the doctor through the rearview mirror. Yuhle was as exhausted as Otto from the all-night drive, but Vivian, who sat in the passenger's seat, had insisted that he get behind the wheel.

Otto thought he knew why. Vivian was a mercenary, and Yuhle was a scientist. Vivian looked fine after her own sleepless night, but she obviously wanted Yuhle to drive so she could keep her hands free.

And that meant she suspected trouble.

Vivian had a 9mm automatic in a holster on her hip, and her purse was filled with grenades. In the trunk of the car, she had stowed a duffel bag filled with a small arsenal of weapons.

Her face remained calm, however, at odds with all the suspicious things she'd been saying before they picked up Dr. Yamazaki. Hell, an hour before, Vivian had had the scientist in the scope of her sniper's rifle when Otto had picked up Dr. Yamazaki at the rendezvous.

For several minutes, there had been silence. It seemed like an hour. Dr. Yamazaki finally broke it.

"So where have you set up base?" she asked.

Yuhle opened his mouth to reply, but Vivian cut him off.

"The desert."

Silence.

"I see," Dr. Yamazaki said.

"So tell me more about this breakout. What else can you remember?" Vivian asked.

Otto shook his head and looked out at the desert passing by. They were on a county road well away from the interstate. No other cars were in sight. Occasionally they passed an isolated ranch or a lonely cluster of dusty trailer homes, but otherwise there was nothing but rocks, scraggly bushes, the occasional lonely mesquite tree, and distant mountains under a brilliant blue sky.

Why was Vivian asking her about that again? She'd told the story of her breakout three times already.

Then it hit him. Vivian was looking for inconsistencies in her story. Otto tuned in as Dr. Yamazaki told about her getaway for the fourth time. He couldn't find anything different from the last three times she'd told it.

So where did that leave them? Believing that a commando squad of Atlanteans had healed her brain, helped her escape, and then conveniently all got killed?

Otto remembered his girlfriend, Jaxon Andersen. She was an Atlantean with no training, and yet she had managed to beat up half a dozen government agents. So yeah, maybe they could have busted her out, but what about healing her brain? Was that even possible? He didn't know much about strokes. He did know that medical researchers had spent years looking for ways to heal the damage and had come up with nothing.

His grandfather, one of the smartest people he had ever known, had suffered a stroke a couple of years ago. Grandpa went from being a whiz at fixing cars and solving crossword puzzles, someone who could quote whole pages from books he had read years before, to a drooling mess in a wheelchair.

Judging from what Yuhle had said, Dr. Yamazaki had been just as bad.

The bleeping of Vivian's phone snapped him out of his thoughts.

She and Otto traded looks. No one was supposed to call except for Grunt or Edward back at base. That ring meant something had gone wrong.

Yuhle had heard it too. He pulled the car off to the side of the road.

"What's going on?" Dr. Yamazaki asked.

"Got to take this call, honey," Vivian said.

Dr. Yamazaki's brow furrowed. "How are you even getting coverage out here?"

"Satellite uplink," Vivian said. Otto noticed she left out the fact that Edward had hacked into a communications satellite so he couldn't be traced. At least that was what Otto presumed he had done. Maybe he was using a different trick. Otto had given up trying to predict what Edward would do.

Once the car came to a stop, Vivian opened the door and stepped out onto the gravel shoulder. Her long blond hair flashed brilliantly in the desert sun, and

Otto couldn't help admiring her athletic body as she stepped away from the car. Reminding himself he had a girlfriend, he looked away.

"Otto, come with me," Vivian called.

Curious, Otto followed.

Vivian walked several yards into the desert, well out of earshot of the car. Otto looked back and saw Yuhle had turned around in his seat and was talking with Dr. Yamazaki. From their expressions, it looked like an argument. The hot desert sun pounded on Otto and made him feel even more tired. Once he caught up with Vivian, she answered the phone.

"What is it, honey?" she asked.

Otto leaned in close to hear the answer. Edward's voice came over the phone. He was a computer hacker and conspiracy theorist who served as the Atlantis Allegiance's eyes and ears. He was also the nerdiest, most paranoid person Otto had ever met.

"Big trouble. Are either of the two scientists there?"

"No, I figured it would be best to do this out of earshot," Vivian replied.

Otto remembered how Dr. Yuhle was insistent before the mission that Dr. Yamazaki would never set up a trap for them, that she was totally dedicated to stopping General Meade and the rest of the secret government project that wanted to enslave the Atlanteans. If Edward didn't want Yuhle to hear what he had to say, then it really was bad news.

Edward went on. "I've picked up some chatter on a military channel in your area. Looks like General Meade's goon squad is closing in on you."

Otto looked all around him, squinting against the harsh southwestern light, hoping to catch a glimpse of a faraway helicopter or vehicle. He saw nothing.

"We got clear of the city without being tailed, I'm sure of it," Vivian said.

"Did you check her for a tracking device?" Edward asked.

"Of course."

Vivian had run a device that looked like an airport security wand up and down Dr. Yamazaki after she had gotten into the car back in Albuquerque.

"Check her again. Visually. General Meade's Poseidon Project has access to all the latest technology. He might have something that resists the detector."

"All right," Vivian said, nervously looking around as Otto had. "How much time do we have?"

"I don't know. I haven't been able to break their code yet. I only know that they're in your area and active."

Vivian sprinted back to the car. Otto hurried to follow.

She yanked open the back door and hauled Dr. Yamazaki out.

"Hey!" the female scientist protested.

"You have a tracking device on you. Know anything about that?" Vivian demanded.

Dr. Yuhle got out of the car. "A tracking device? Nonsense."

"Stay out of this," Vivian snapped. Otto was taken aback. Normally she was all sugar and spice. Right then, though, she looked as if she wanted to tear someone's head off. He had to remind himself that the woman was a mercenary, and from the hints she'd dropped, she had once been an assassin.

Dr. Yamazaki was wearing a man's trench coat over a cheap old dress and even cheaper shoes. She had claimed that she had taken the wallet from one of her dying saviors and bought some clothes at Goodwill to replace her hospital robe. That part of her story certainly appeared to be true.

Vivian tore off the trench coat and handed it to Otto.

"Take a good look at this, inside and out. I'm going to take her over behind that mesquite tree and check out the rest of her. No peeking, boys."

"I'm not trying to trap you," Dr. Yamazaki protested.

"She'd never do that," Yuhle said, trying to get between them.

"Hey, Yuhle," Otto said. "We got company coming soon. Take the binoculars in the glove compartment, get on top of the car, and take a look around."

Yuhle turned pale. He looked at his old boss as Vivian hustled her away, he hesitated, and then he ran for the car.

Otto nodded. Yuhle didn't always think straight, but he seemed to appreciate how much danger they were all in. He'd been part of General Meade's Poseidon Project and knew better than any of them how determined and ruthless that man could be.

Otto turned his attention to the trench coat, not really sure what he was searching for. What did a tracking device look like, anyway? First he rummaged through the pockets and found them all empty. He felt along the lining of the coat as he'd once seen in a gangster movie but didn't find any suspicious lumps.

Yuhle clambered up onto the roof of the car, the thin metal groaning in protest, and scanned the horizon.

"See anything?" Otto asked.

"Not yet," Yuhle said, slowly turning a full one hundred eighty degrees. When he moved to face Vivian, who was giving a loudly protesting Dr. Yamazaki a strip search behind the mesquite tree, Yuhle practically jumped in the air and turned away.

"No, I didn't see anything. Nothing at all, got that?" Yuhle said, turning red from something other than the desert heat.

"Ah...right," Otto said and went back to searching the trench coat.

He patted it, turned it inside out, then inside in, and still didn't find anything.

A minute later, he found it by pure chance. As he was turning the trench coat over, his hand passed over something that didn't feel like fabric. A small circular area the size of his thumbnail felt smooth, like plastic. He held it up to the light and squinted.

He saw a patch of clear plastic that contained a tiny spiderweb of circuits and wires. Even staring straight at it, he could barely make it out. If he hadn't accidentally touched it, he wouldn't have spotted it in a million years.

"I found it!" he called out.

Vivian came running. A moment later, Dr. Yamazaki emerged from behind the tree, buttoning up her dress.

Vivian studied the little patch, then peeled it off, dropped it in the gritty soil, and ground it back and forth with her shoe.

"That ought to wreck it," she said.

Everyone turned to Dr. Yamazaki, who stood uncertainly in the road.

"Care to explain this?" Vivian demanded.

Dr. Yamazaki's eyes went wide.

"I-I didn't know! They must have put it on me."

"When?"

"How should I know? Maybe in the motel last night, maybe in the diner this morning."

Yuhle cut in. "It was on the back of her coat. That's where I'd put it if I was planting one on her. If I was planting it on myself, I'd hide it inside a sleeve or something."

Otto looked back and forth between them, not sure who to believe.

Vivian pulled the automatic pistol from the holster at her belt and pointed it at Dr. Yamazaki.

"Whoa, wait a minute!" Otto shouted.

Vivian ignored him. "Care to tell us who sent you to trap us?"

Dr. Yamazaki stood there, trembling, unable to speak.

Otto put himself between the two women.

"Look, everyone. Calm down. Vivian, please point that somewhere else. If they were going to attack us, they would have done so already."

Vivian shook her head. "They would hang back and follow us to our base to get the entire Atlantis Allegiance."

Otto thought for a moment. "Okay, that makes sense, but now that you've broken that thing..."

Yuhle put his binoculars back up to his eyes and scanned the horizon.

"Dust cloud on the road behind us!"

He spun forward and paused a moment.

"And ahead!"

Vivian sprinted to the car, popped the trunk, and grabbed a large duffel bag that Otto knew was filled with guns.

"Everyone in the car!" Otto shouted. "We can have this argument later. We need to survive the next ten minutes first!"

Chapter 2

JUNE 17, 2016, LOS ANGELES,
CALIFORNIA

8:30 PM

Jaxon Ares Andersen sighed as she read the website of the *Los Angeles Times* as part of her summer school homework. Students had to read a newspaper article and then write an essay on it.

Boring, but on the other hand totally difficult.

No one seemed to care that she was dyslexic. Oh, there was a special counselor at school who was oh-so-helpful in that way people could be that made them look saintly and her look stupid, and her foster parents said all the usual supportive and encouraging things, but that didn't keep her teacher from assigning her just as much reading and writing as everyone else.

"Why couldn't I just be a gardener?" she grumbled under her breath as she tried to focus on the words scrambling before her eyes. "I'm the best gardener in the world."

Jaxon gave a nervous look over her shoulder to make sure no one had heard. She sat at her desk in her room, using one of the Grants' laptops. No one stood at the open doorway to her room who could have caught what she had said. The house was so huge she could have probably shouted that and gotten away with it.

Still, she should control her mouth. If the Grants learned about her weird abilities with plants, there could be trouble. Stephen Grant, her foster father, was a plant pathologist. If he found out, he'd probably want to conduct scientific tests on her or something, turn her into a guinea pig. All she wanted was to be left alone.

She sighed and went back to reading the paper, or at least trying to. The headlines were all the usual boring stuff—political fights between important people she'd never heard of, some new highway construction project that was tying up commuter traffic, people complaining about the harsh fines the city had put in place against wasting water, more depressing news about California's endless drought...it was all the same stuff as the last time she had been given the assignment a week ago. She had suspected that her class was going to get that assignment every week. Wonderful. Then an odd headline caught her eye.

MYSTERIOUS TEENAGE SUPERHERO SAVES SENIOR CITIZEN

LAPD have reported a strange incident last night.

Mrs. Maria Rosales, 71, was walking home from a bus stop in East LA when she was accosted by two men who demanded her purse. Before she could react, a young man wearing sweatpants and a hooded sweatshirt attacked her would-be muggers and knocked them down with a series of martial arts moves.

He then walked Mrs. Rosales home and fled the scene.

Rosales was unhurt and described the attacker as a young white male in his mid-teens.

"He barely spoke," Rosales said. "He only asked if I was all right. He sounded educated and definitely Anglo, although I didn't get a good look at him. God bless him."

This is the third such report in the past few weeks. The first occurred on May 13, when a man in a wheelchair reported being saved from a mugger by a teenager. On June 1, two teenaged girls walking in a shopping mall parking lot reported a similar incident of being rescued from a man who tried to force them into a car. In both cases, the vigilante matched the description of the teen described in the latest case. All three incidents happened in the hours of darkness.

Police ombudsman Jerome Clarke stated yesterday, "While we ask all citizens to be vigilant in spotting and promptly reporting crime, we do not condone the actions of this young man. What he is doing is highly dangerous and could result in his serious *injury. It's best to leave police work to the police."*

Police have no suspects in any of the three cases.

Jaxon sat back, her eyes smarting from trying to puzzle through the words.

Well, that sure was a different story. At least that one was interesting, although a bit weird. She started working on her essay, gritting her teeth as the word processor underlined practically every word with an angry red squiggle.

It took her an hour to finish the essay and wrestle with the spell checker to make sure all the words were correct. Spell checkers offered alternate words depending on what the user typed, perfect for people who didn't have dyslexia. If the mind mixed up the letters of everything that was read, though, then the computer might not offer the correct word, and if it offered more than one choice, the user was sunk.

And sometimes, Jaxon's spelling was so horrible the spell checker had no idea what she was trying to write.

A knock on her doorframe made her jump. She turned to see Isadore Grant, her foster mother, standing in the doorway. She was a glamorous woman in her forties who had made her fortune in disaster insurance. Jaxon hadn't heard her approach. Isadore had a freaky habit of making no sound when she walked, and Jaxon got the impression that she had been standing there for a while. It wasn't the first time Isadore had snuck up on her like that.

"All done with your homework?" Isadore asked.

"Yep. Thanks for letting me use the Internet."

The Grants didn't let her get online unless she needed to for homework. It was one of their million rules. They had some dumb idea of living an all-natural life and staying away from electronic media and processed food. It didn't stop them from living in a mansion in the middle of the biggest, most polluted city in the country, though. Adults had a habit of making convenient exceptions to their morals in order to get what they wanted.

"You're really getting through your homework quickly now. That's great!" Isadore said in that faux friendly tone she had. She was usually as cold as ice, but she did seem to be making a conscious effort to be nice to Jaxon in her own awkward way. "Once you've sent in your assignment, bring me the laptop. It's time to go to bed."

Jaxon looked at the clock. It was barely past nine, but she knew it would be pointless to argue. There was nothing to do in that house anyway. No TV, no Internet, the Grants had taken her phone...she might as well go to bed.

Half an hour later, she lay wide awake in her darkened room, waiting for sleep to come. She thought about how different her life was compared with a month before, and how much it was the same. The Grant home was only the latest in a series of foster homes. It was by far the richest—the Grants were multimillion-aires—but in the end, it was just another hotel.

She couldn't count how many foster homes she'd been in. Some had been okay, and some had been terrible. The Grants were in the middle. Stephen Grant didn't check out her body or try to get close to her as some foster fathers had, and they weren't religious nuts like some of the other placements, and yet there was something disturbing about those two. They were like actors playing a part. They obviously didn't want a child of their own and had never adopted, so why had they volunteered to be foster parents? It turned out she was their first foster child.

She wanted to know why they had decided to take her, but something prevented her from asking. The Grants were secretive sometimes. Several rooms in the house were off limits, and the Grants were vague about their past and their work. Jaxon had the feeling that if she asked why those two busy, antisocial people had volunteered to be foster parents, she wouldn't get an honest answer.

She missed her last group home. As with the foster homes, she'd been in countless group homes. She was always getting shifted from one place to another because she was a "problem child." At sixteen, though, she wasn't a child, and the problems were all other people's fault. People picked on her because she was mixed race, or because she was the new kid, or mostly because she didn't quite fit in. It was as though they sensed she was different from anybody else, even though she had done her best to hide her unusual powers.

Her last placement, at the Forever Welcome Group Home, had been no different at first. A snobbish girl with the usual flock of followers had singled her out and made her life hell. That was nothing new. There was someone like that in every new school or group home.

But there had been something different about that place too. She'd gotten her first boyfriend, Otto Heike. He'd accepted her from the start, and the two had grown close so quickly. She hadn't even had a chance to kiss him before it all fell apart.

Otto had been in the group home because he was a pyromaniac. He was as addicted to setting fires as some at her new school were addicted to cocaine. It gave him a rush and took him away from his problems. He seemed pretty normal to Jaxon, though. Maybe all he needed was to get away from his nasty parents to get better. She'd met them once. If she had had to grow up with that pair, she'd have wanted to get addicted to something too. Anything would be better than having to deal with those two.

They were always trying to find fault with Otto, and they sure got their chance a couple of weeks ago. A lance of pain went right through her heart as she thought about it.

Jaxon was finally finding a place to belong, finally coming out of her shell with someone she liked and felt she could trust, and then disaster struck. It was during the visitation weekend, when the parents who bothered to come could have a big picnic with their messed-up kids, and everyone would paste on smiles and pretend they cared about each other. Otto had wanted to get away from his mother and father, who had only shown up for the sake of appearances, and so they went to the greenhouse.

Jaxon had loved that place, although as with everything else, her love was mixed with dread. She had been doing some gardening therapy in order to calm her nerves, and while she was handling the plants, she had discovered a new ability beyond the super strength she already knew she had. She could make plants grow just by touching them. She had shared that secret with Otto, the only person she had ever told about how truly different she was.

Otto was amazed but didn't reject her or run away in fear. It made her realize that she didn't have to be alone for the rest of her life.

They had gone to the greenhouse so she could get away from the bullies and he could get away from his unloving parents. Jaxon's heart had been racing. She thought that if she was ever going to get her first kiss, it would be then.

And then they'd been attacked. Six burly men had tried to abduct her. Why, she didn't know. Of course girls got kidnapped sometimes. There was no shortage of perverts out there, but they usually grabbed a girl in some isolated place. She'd never heard of six guys breaking into the grounds of a group home to carry off one of the residents.

They had to fight them off. Otto had tried to help, but it was Jaxon who did most of the work. She had the strength of an NFL linebacker and the speed of a black belt. She'd knocked all of them flat, and she and Otto had run to get help.

By the time they had alerted the group home staff, the greenhouse was in flames.

Of course no one believed their unbe-lievable story. Of course they blamed Otto.

Otto was already eighteen, so he got sent to prison. Jaxon, knowing those men would come back for her and fearing for her life, had gotten her roommate, Ginger, to make some calls to people she knew in Child Protective Services and get her reassigned.

So there she was, in a cold mansion with its cold occupants, pretending to be grateful for getting to go to an exclusive school filled with coke fiends and snobs. She was alone again. She was alone, as usual.

So what was in her future? More of the same? Jaxon didn't see what else she could do.

Her thoughts went back to that kid who was running around the city at night, stopping crime. He sounded as messed up and alone as she was. No one pulled a stunt like that unless they were pretty out there. But at least he was doing something useful.

The paper said he knew martial arts. She was studying that too. It could come in handy if those men came looking for her again.

The house had gone quiet. Stephen and Isadore usually turned in early. She couldn't see any light coming from under the crack in her door.

A strange feeling came over her, a restless energy that was so unlike her usual depressed laziness.

Jaxon got up and parted the blinds. The lights in the greenhouse were off. Stephen wasn't working late as he sometimes did. The house had a large backyard screened with trees to give the illusion that the place was out in the country. The trick worked if someone was standing on the lawn, but if she looked out a second-story window as she was doing then, she could see the lights of Los Angeles twinkling through the branches. Not far off, a highway ran like a bright ribbon through the night, the lights of the cars making an almost continuous glowing line. A whole city was out there, and she was stuck inside.

Jaxon turned away from the view in disgust. What a boring life she lived. She had all sorts of strange powers, as if she were a mutant or a superhero or something, yet all she had ever been was some orphan, some high school loser.

On impulse, she walked to a corner of her room and bent forward. After placing her hands on the floor, she edged her feet up the wall until she had almost all her weight on her two hands, her toes barely touching the wall.

Not too impressive. Lots of kids in gym class could do that. But how about something a bit harder?

She centered one hand and pulled the other away. Her body wavered for a moment until she found her equilibrium. Jaxon pulled one foot away from the wall so that even more weight was on her one hand.

The only thing challenging about that was keeping balance. Her arm barely felt the strain at all.

Just how strong was she, anyway? When she was nine, she had broken the wrist of one of her foster fathers for trying to mess with her. That had gotten her labeled a problem child. It had also made her fear her powers and hide them. She had learned her lesson—being different only got her in trouble.

So she had never really tested the limits of her abilities. Steadying herself, she flexed the fingers of her hand until she was holding herself up on her fingertips.

Impressive. Maybe some gymnast or yoga master could do that, but not the average high schooler.

How far could she go?

One by one, she pulled her fingers away. Her eyes went wide with astonishment when she pulled them all away except for her index finger. It held up her entire weight, its tip white with the pressure.

A sharp crack sounded beneath her, then came a pain in her finger, and she tumbled. On instinct, she somersaulted and landed on her feet, then brought her finger to her mouth and tasted blood.

She looked down at the floor and saw she had poked a hole through the wood. She'd put too much weight on too little space and punched through the floor. She was lucky she hadn't broken her finger.

Or maybe her finger was unbreakable. She'd never broken a bone before. She'd never even had a sprained ankle.

She could bleed, though. Her finger had a big gash down the side. Jaxon was not invulnerable.

Still sucking on the wound, she crept to the doorway and listened. No one was coming, unless Isadore was spying on her again.

Jaxon opened the door a crack. The hallway was shrouded in darkness. It looked as though her little stunt hadn't woken up her foster parents. She'd need to think up an excuse for the hole in the floor, though.

She tiptoed to the bathroom to get a bandage. As an experiment, she actually walked on the tips of her toes. It didn't tire her at all.

In a few minutes, she was back in bed, her finger wrapped in a bandage, her mind whirling with possibilities.

I could teach that vigilante a thing or two about fighting, she thought.

It took her a long time to fall asleep.

Chapter 3

JUNE 17, 2016, MOJAVE DESERT, NEVADA

12:05 PM

Yuhle slammed on the gas, and the Subaru tore down the isolated county road. The dust cloud behind them loomed closer. Otto peered out the back window and could see it was pretty big, as if it was being made by more than one vehicle. Up ahead rose another dust cloud, smaller and more distant.

"We're trapped!" Otto shouted. "What do we do?"

"Fight. What do you think?" Vivian said. She bent over the duffel bag at her feet and pulled out a compact Uzi submachine gun.

"You're going to shoot them? They're American government agents," Otto said, shocked.

"They're going to shoot us. What do you suggest I do, honey, blow them a kiss?"

"Can't we just stun them with our Tasers or something?" Otto said. He reached under his seat and pulled out the Taser that Grunt had trained him to use. The hulking mercenary had trained Yuhle as well, and Otto knew that an identical Taser sat under the driver's seat.

"That would be nice, honey, but I don't think they'll get close enough for that. They'll shoot at us from a distance. No need to get up close and personal."

"Then we should surrender," Otto objected. "I don't want us all to die."

"Surrendering is the best way to make sure we all do die," Yuhle said, his face set in grim determination. He'd put his foot on the gas, and the Subaru shot down the narrow two-lane county road. The dust cloud behind them grew closer, however, and Otto could make out a gleam of metal in the distance.

"They're going to catch us," Dr. Yamazaki said. "Give me a gun."

"No way," Vivian said, giving her a hard look. "I'm not a hundred percent on you yet, girl."

Otto pulled his Taser from under his seat and opened the window. He could see that there were actually two vehicles behind them, white Range Rovers with powerful engines that made their little Subaru look puny and pathetic by comparison. The Range Rovers were gaining fast.

Otto looked at the stun gun in his hand and suddenly felt inadequate. While he was only an okay shot with it, he had never fired at a living target. And how was he supposed to hit someone inside a car anyway?

Vivian must have noticed his expression because she nudged him in the shoulder. When he turned, she dumped the contents of her purse in his lap—a half dozen grenades.

He'd been trained in those too. Otto checked the color-coded dots on the bottom to see what kind they were. Two had black dots showing they were tear gas grenades, three more had yellow dots showing they were flash and stun grenades, and one had the red dot that told him it was an incendiary grenade.

Otto's heart pounded as he gazed at the little black metal sphere. He looked at Vivian and saw she was busy loading her Uzi. She had been in such a hurry she must not have realized she had given him the firebomb. He held it, enchanted at the possibilities. His mouth went dry, and his vision became hazy. So much fire...

Yuhle jerked on the wheel and brought him back to his senses. Puffs of grit and pavement burst in a regular line in front of the car. It took a moment for Otto to figure out what he was seeing.

Impacts from bullets. Their pursuers were shooting at them!

He turned in his seat. From the passenger's seat of the leading Range Rover, a man in a black suit was leaning out the window and firing with some sort of automatic weapon. The steady flare of the muzzle was like a flame. But not the kind of flame Otto liked. That flame was trying to kill him.

Yuhle swerved again, trying to take evasive action, but had little room to maneuver on such a narrow road. Bullets plinked off the rear and roof. One took off the side view mirror.

To his credit, Yuhle didn't waver. The scientist hunkered down in his seat and kept weaving back and forth, doing what little he could to keep them alive. It was up to the other members of the team to do more.

Vivian opened her window and readied her Uzi. Otto was quicker. He leaned out his already open window, pulled the pin of a tear gas grenade, and tossed it in the path of the oncoming Range Rovers. The little metal orb bounced along the road and burst, sending a thick cloud of yellowish smoke over the entire road and blotting the pursuing vehicles from view.

Otto let out a cheer and pumped his fist to the sky, then stopped as the vehicles drove right through the gas.

"You got to do more than that, honey!" Vivian shouted. "They're going too fast to catch more than a whiff of that."

Otto took a flash and stun grenade and tossed that next. It burst just in front of the lead vehicle, the one from which the gunner was still leaning, replacing the magazine on his machine gun to give them another burst of bullets.

After a blinding flash, the gunner jerked and dropped his weapon. The driver swerved, and the Range Rover took a sharp turn, went off the road, smashed through some bushes, and bumped over the hard ground before slamming to a stop against a large rock.

"Whoa! I hope everyone is all right," Otto said.

"You're too nice for this game, honey." Vivian laughed. "They won't be so nice to you."

She leaned out the window and gave a burst of fire against the second vehicle. It swerved and slowed but didn't stop.

"Car ahead!" Yuhle shouted.

Otto turned and saw a car parked parallel to the road, blocking both lanes. Two men in black suits stood behind the front—Otto remembered Grunt telling him that the engine block was the only bulletproof part of a car—leveling their pistols in their direction.

Both pistols flashed. A bullet smashed the windshield. Otto felt it rush past him before it exited the rear window.

Otto shouted something that would have gotten him a demerit at the group home. Dr. Yamazaki was saying the same thing, in fact a whole string of incredibly creative swear words, including a couple Otto wasn't sure he knew the meanings to. He reminded himself to ask her about them if they survived.

That depended on Yuhle's driving. He swerved off the road, missed a mesquite tree by inches, took a sharp turn to avoid a boulder, and then got back on the road just as the two men who had tried to form a roadblock turned and fired again. One bullet added another hole in the rear window. The other smashed through a taillight.

The two men scrambled to get in their Range Rover. The other Range Rover swerved around them and continued the chase. Otto grabbed a grenade, pulled the pin, and threw it. As soon as he did, he realized that in his panic, he hadn't checked what kind it was.

A blossom of flame erupted in the road. Otto's eyes went wide. He hadn't realized the incendiary bomb would be so powerful. The pursuing vehicle rolled right through it then emerged cocooned in fire.

To his amazement, the flames didn't blow out with the speed of the Range Rover. They clung to it, peeling back the paint and buckling the windshield. Even the tires were on fire, flames spinning like Fourth of July fireworks.

The Range Rover screeched to a halt behind them. Doors on both sides opened, and the occupants leaped out before rolling on the ground to douse the flames on their clothes and then sprinting away from their vehicle.

A moment later, Otto understood why they ran. The gas tank lit, and once again there was a giant explosion. The third vehicle, which had been trying to pass the explosion, had to career out of the way and got stuck in a ditch.

Otto stared, leaning far out the window. Someone was saying something, but he didn't hear. The wind whipped through his hair and roared in his ears, but he barely noticed. The flaming car was so beautiful, a halo of fire crowned by a blackening cloud rising high above it, all of it backlit by the original explosion of his firebomb, which still burned brilliantly in the road a couple of hundred yards behind. He had never seen a flame so big in his life. It was even grander than the barn he had burned down.

A strong hand grabbed his shoulder and yanked him into the car. Vivian.

She gave him a disgusted look, and suddenly he felt like a schoolkid caught looking at dirty websites. Vivian stared at him for a full minute, but he couldn't look her in the eye.

At last she turned around to face forward.

"My mistake," she whispered with her back to him. "I didn't realize what I was giving you. Well, at least they won't be chasing us anytime soon."

Otto hung his head.

At least no one got killed, he added silently. At least she didn't call me "Pyro" like Grunt and Edward do.

Even that didn't make him feel better.

After a few more minutes of silence, Dr. Yamazaki spoke up. "They tried to kill me along with the rest of you. Do you trust me now?"

"Of course," Yuhle said.

"We'll see," Vivian said. "They could have set you up and then just stabbed you in the back."

"They already did that when they induced a stroke in my brain," Dr. Yamazaki said.

Otto looked at her curiously. "So how did the Atlanteans heal you?"

Dr. Yamazaki got a faraway look. "I'm not sure. My mind was all muddled. I remember a group of them coming into my hospital room. They all had that mixed-race look that Atlanteans have."

"Black skin with blue eyes and kinda Asian features?" Otto said, remembering his girlfriend, Jaxon. She felt she was ugly, but he thought she looked great. Was he ever going to see her again?

Dr. Yamazaki nodded. "One of them put her hands on my head, and within a few minutes, my motor control improved, and my thoughts began to clear. It was hard to keep track during the chase, but the time between her laying hands on me and my ending up having to drive a car and then escape on foot couldn't have been more than half an hour. It was probably considerably less than that."

"So they just rewired your brain and healed the damage with a touch? That sounds magical," Otto said.

The scientist shook her head. "There's no such thing as magic. Everything has a scientific explanation."

"So what's the scientific explanation for that?"

Dr. Yamazaki shrugged, looking completely at a loss. Otto guessed that she didn't get that look very often.

"Jaxon has a magical ability too," Otto said. "She showed me when we were in the group home together. She—"

"That's enough, honey," Vivian cut in from the front seat.

"What's wrong with telling her?" Otto asked.

"Figure it out," Vivian said, her voice cutting.

Dr. Yamazaki hung her head. Yuhle gave Vivian a frown.

Even if Dr. Yamazaki isn't a spy, she's dividing the Atlantis Allegiance just by showing up, Otto thought.

Vivian got back on the phone and called Edward.

"We're clear," she said. "Prepare to evacuate and meet at the rendezvous."

Then she tossed the phone out the window.

She turned back and smiled at Otto. "Don't litter. It's bad karma, except when your phone signal can be triangulated. We don't want them converging on us again."

"Why did you tell him to evacuate the base? They'll never find us there. It's in the middle of nowhere."

"We were in the middle of nowhere here, and they found us, honey," Vivian said. "Plus they saw the direction we were going. Judging from that, they'd probably figure we'd set up somewhere in the Nevada desert. They could spread out and search for us. The desert is big, but not that big. Sooner or later, they'd find us."

Otto's heart fell. Was any place safe? And how were they going to save Jaxon if they were on the run themselves? She wouldn't be any safer with them than with her fake foster parents.

"So what's this rendezvous?" he asked at last.

Yuhle answered. "An emergency meeting place we have in Arizona near the Mexican border. It's just as remote as our old place, and Grunt has some friends there."

"Well, I'm not sure I'd call them friends." Vivian chuckled.

Yuhle shrugged and adjusted his glasses. "Friendly, in any case. And we have a shortage of people like that in our lives."

"So why didn't you tell me about all this?" Otto asked.

"The less you know, the better, honey," Vivian said. "General Meade's men would be happy to torture you if you ever fell into their hands."

"How could he do that? I'm not some terrorist, and this isn't Guantanamo!"

Yuhle sighed. He took a turn onto a different county road and sped up on the straightaway.

"You need to realize that not everyone in the government is a good guy, kid," he said. "You seem to think General Meade is some maverick. He isn't. When I was working for the Poseidon Project, he was having a hard time convincing his superiors that researching the Atlantis gene was worth it, but the high command at the Pentagon had no problem with him doing illegal wiretaps, monitoring civilians, or kidnapping. He can do anything he wants as long as he gives the Pentagon results."

"Even give a citizen a stroke and turn her into a vegetable," Dr. Yamazaki whispered.

Otto shuddered. It had all seemed so abstract, him hanging out in the desert with a group of hackers and mercenaries playing at being revolutionaries. But then it hit home. He couldn't rely on the law or the Constitution or even common human decency. There was a government within the government, and he and his friends were at war with it.

He couldn't expect mercy in war.

Chapter 4

JUNE 18, 2016, LOS ANGELES, CALIFORNIA

10:30 AM

Jaxon slumped down the hall, heading for her locker to prepare for yet another dull day of summer school. Except for a few snide looks from some of Courtney's friends, everyone passing by in the hallway ignored her.

Better than usual, Jaxon thought. *At this rate, I'll be the most popular girl in the class by 2050.*

She found her locker and grabbed the latch. Jaxon jerked her hand away as she felt something slick and greasy smear her hand.

A burst of laughter echoed down the hall. Courtney and a gaggle of her followers stood a few yards away, mocking her. Their little plastic-surgery noses turned up at her in contempt.

Jaxon glared at them and then looked at her locker. Once she was paying attention, she could see it was coated with a thin layer of…something.

I definitely don't want to know what this stuff is.

The laughter continued, along with whispers all around her. Even kids not in Courtney's little army of cokehead followers stood there grinning. Jaxon felt like a fuse that was burning down to a keg of dynamite. She had a vision of beating up every single one of those spoiled rich kids and leaving them groaning on the floor. Her fists clenched. Jaxon took several deep breaths, trying to control herself.

Why should I control myself?

On impulse, she opened Courtney's locker, which was next to hers.

"Hey!" Courtney shouted. "Get out of there!"

Jaxon ignored her and rummaged through the locker. What a mess. Books were tumbled in a heap, with random papers and old homework assignments and tests crumpled together. Tossing out a few Fs and Ds and sweeping aside some old makeup, she found what she was looking for—a scarf.

A hand grabbed her shoulder and tried to spin her around. Jaxon resisted and was surprised that she actually had to put some effort in it. Courtney was stronger than she looked. Must have been the cocaine.

"What are you doing, freak?" Courtney shouted in a shrill voice, right next to her ear.

"Don't give me a headache," Jaxon replied in as calm a voice as she could, keeping her back to the bully. She held the scarf up, having to jerk to the side to keep Courtney from grabbing it. "I have to say you really do know how to accessorize. Can I borrow this?"

Jaxon started wiping her locker clean with Courtney's scarf. The whole hallway burst out in laughter again, but not at Jaxon that time.

"You bitch!" Courtney yelled, and she raked her fingernails across Jaxon's cheek.

Jaxon flicked her hand away, the movement so fast, so automatic, that she didn't have time to pull back on her strength.

"Ow!" Courtney shouted, holding her hand.

Jaxon looked at her for a moment, concerned. She hadn't broken anything, had she? The last time she accidentally broke someone's bones, it cost her years of trouble.

No, Courtney's hand was a bit red, but since it was clenched in rage and flying at her face, it couldn't be too hurt.

Once again, Jaxon reacted automatically, using an aikido move she'd learned from Marquis. She grabbed Courtney's fist, deflected the blow, and used the girl's own momentum to spin her around like a ballerina doing a pirouette.

Courtney staggered and backed up, fear flickering across her usually arrogant features.

Jaxon purposely turned her back on the cheap bully for a second time and finished cleaning her locker with the scarf. Then she used a dry part of the material to wipe off her fingers.

"You're dead," Courtney whispered and stalked off, her blond hair flouncing as she broke through the circle of leering kids.

Jaxon was tempted to put the greasy scarf back in Courtney's locker, after smearing all the contents of course, but decided against it. That had gone far enough. Instead, she dropped it on the floor.

She gathered all her books—no way she was going to risk leaving anything in her locker after that little scene—and headed for class. As she passed through the crowd, she secretly enjoyed all the approving looks she was suddenly getting. Was that all it took to be popular, being as nasty as Courtney? Maybe the school coke dealer and self-proclaimed "most beautiful girl in school" wasn't as popular as she thought.

Class was boring, as usual. At least it gave her a chance to calm her nerves. The teacher was droning on about American history and the Bill of Rights. Jaxon wondered if there was anything in it about the right to be left alone. A fight made her feel all wired and a bit ill, even when she won. She didn't really care if no one liked her. She was used to that. Who cared what people like Courtney thought anyway? It was the constant harassment that got to her. It wore her down, year in and year out. When would it stop? Would she have to actually break someone's wrist as she did with Mr. Spencer? Was violence the only way to make the wolves stop circling?

Something the teacher said caught her attention.

"Now let's take turns each reading a paragraph from the Bill of Rights."

Oh great. Reading. She could toss grown men and hold herself up with one finger, but she read like a first grader who had been hit over the head with a Tonka truck.

"Courtney, could you read first?"

Jaxon let out a relieved sigh.

Courtney began to read in a bored voice, "Amendment One: Congress shall make no law respecting an establish-ment of religion, or prohibiting the free exercise thereof; or abridging the freedom of speech, or of the press; or the right of the people peaceably to assemble, and to petition the government for a redress of grievances."

Does "redress of grievances" mean I get to complain to the government about Courtney? Jaxon wondered.

"Thank you, Courtney. Brett, could you go next, please?"

Jaxon looked over at Brett and saw he had nodded off.

"Brett! Could you wake up and join the class?" the teacher snapped.

Brett's head jerked up. He stared at the teacher for a moment, his face slack with confusion, and then his eyes cleared, and he started reading.

"Amendment One: Congress shall make no law respecting—"

"Second amendment, please." The teacher sighed.

The class laughed again. Jaxon giggled. She couldn't believe she had gone on a date with that guy. But at least he'd treated her nicer than everyone else. Had to watch those hands, though.

The teacher went through each amendment, selecting a student to read each of them. They were almost through, and Jaxon was beginning to think she was going to make it when...

"Jaxon, could you read the next one, please?"

Jaxon tensed. Her teacher knew she was dyslexic, so why was she putting her through that? With a sigh, Jaxon tried to read.

"Amendment Nine: The en... emulation..."

"Enumeration," her teacher corrected.

"The enumeration in the Congress..."

"Constitution."

Giggles started sounding around her. Jaxon felt her face going red.

"...the Constitution, for civil rights..."

"...of certain rights," her teacher said. More giggles. The teacher glared around the room, but the giggles didn't stop.

"...still nobody constructed..."

"...shall not be construed..."

More giggles. The people in front of her kept glancing over their shoulders and grinning. Jaxon didn't look at Courtney or Brett. She didn't want to see the expressions on their faces.

Jaxon took a deep breath and continued.

"...to delay or dis...dis..."

"...to deny or disparage others retained by the people," the teacher finished for her. "Thank you, Jaxon. That will be all."

"Oh my God, she's like totally useless," Courtney whispered loud enough for everyone to hear.

"Knock that off, whoever that was," the teacher snapped.

A few more giggles erupted around the room.

Jaxon stared at her desk, burning with shame. She could hear their laughter ringing in her ears long after they had stopped.

That night, Jaxon lay in her bed again, feeling restless. She knew she wouldn't fall asleep for a long time. By all rights, she should feel happy in her new place. Despite the strict rules, she had a good thing going there—a huge house, her own plot of vegetables in the greenhouse to relax with, okay foster parents who actually seemed to give a damn. What else could she want?

Friends and a place to belong, Jaxon thought.

Not as if that had ever been a part of her life except for those precious few weeks in the group home with Otto. She'd always been the outsider. Shouldn't she just get used to it?

Why should I get used to it? Why do I have to settle for second best?

Something Courtney had said kept coming back to haunt her, cutting into her heart like a razor blade.

Useless. She said I was useless.

The worst of it all was that Courtney was right. What had Jaxon ever done that was of use to anybody? She was some sort of medical miracle, some sort of superwoman, and yet all she did was go to school, get bad grades, and get rejected by a bunch of superficial idiots.

She sat up in bed. Useless, useless, useless. Well, what could she do? She was just a kid.

No she wasn't, she was a superwoman with magical powers. Who else could make plants grow simply by touching them? Who else could do push-ups on one finger?

Who else could punch through a wooden floor with their fingertip? She'd told Isadore that she'd lifted up her chair and it had slipped from her grasp, and one of the legs punched a hole in the floor. It was a bogus excuse, and Isadore didn't look convinced, but at least she hadn't bugged Jaxon about it. All Jaxon wanted was to be left alone.

You sit around all your life like a blob, hoping everything will pass you by, when what you really want to do is hit back at all the meanness in the world.

Something her yoga instructor, Juliette, had told her came back to her. It was a line from some book called *The Gnostic Gospels*.

"If you let what is inside of you out of you, what is inside of you will save you. If you don't let what is inside of you out of you, what is inside of you will kill you."

Jaxon sat up in bed. If she kept denying what she was, if she kept hiding all her life, all she could look forward to was another seventy years of the same. No way was she going to let that happen.

But what to do? Revealing her powers would be dangerous. Those guys who had tried to abduct her back at the group home had obviously come after her because they knew about her special abilities. There was no other explanation. They had come for her, not Otto, and if they had wanted to abduct any ordinary girl, they could have done it more easily by prowling the backstreets and looking for someone walking alone. The whole thing looked like a planned operation.

How can you be yourself when being yourself is dangerous?

Jaxon got out of bed, her mind racing. Sleep wouldn't come for hours. She tiptoed to her door and listened. The house was quiet, the Grants having gone to bed early again. She moved to her dresser, put on a pair of jeans and a shirt, plus a hooded sweatshirt, and went to her window.

She opened it and looked out over the twinkling carpet of lights that was Los Angeles. The lawn lay far below. Even though she was only on the second floor, the mansion had soaring ceilings that made it seem as if she was on the fourth floor.

So what? She'd punched through a wooden floor with her fingertip.

She put a leg out the window, then swung the other out until she was sitting on the ledge.

Don't think. Just do.

She took a deep breath and jumped. She landed with a soft thud on the grass below. Her legs barely flexed, and she didn't feel any pain. She took a couple of experimental steps and found that she hadn't sprained or strained anything.

Let's see a normal person do that, she thought. *Good thing I'm not suicidal. I'd never be able to manage it!*

With a chuckle, Jaxon sprinted across the lawn, leaped the wrought-iron fence on instinct, and soared a full ten feet in the air. She landed on the other side, as if she had been jumping over a soda can on the sidewalk, and ran into the night.

"Time to get useful," she said as the cool night air enveloped her, and the lights of Los Angeles spread before her. It would all be hers.

Chapter 5

JUNE 18, 2016, ALBUQUERQUE,
NEW MEXICO

1:15 PM

General Meade was beginning to think he was the only competent person in the entire United States government. His agents had utterly failed to stop the group led by Dr. Yuhle, the former Poseidon Project employee, from taking away Dr. Yamazaki. Yuhle or someone with him had found the tracking device, destroyed it, and fought off his agents. So not only had he lost the one person who was the leading expert on the Atlantis gene, but also from all reports it appeared she had recovered from that stroke he'd given her.

How? It must have been that band of Atlanteans who had sprung her out of the hospital. Yuhle couldn't have cured her. He was a decent scientist, but no one knew how to heal a brain ravaged by stroke. It could only have been a special power by one of those Atlanteans.

General Meade rubbed his jaw and stared at the wall of his office, past the photos of himself as a younger man in various theaters of war or the one showing him receiving a medal from the previous president. Instead, he looked off into his own imagination, wondering about the two groups fighting against him.

The Atlanteans, for all their special abilities, had acted like amateurs. Even his blundering goon squad had managed to kill them, except for one they'd wounded and captured. He'd have to pry some information out of him about how many were in his group and what they were planning to do next. They surely hadn't sent their entire force against him the other day. There would be more, and they would be less confident and more cautious next time. That would make them harder to beat.

The other group, the one Dr. Yuhle had started, was proving tougher. They seemed to anticipate his every move. They must have had a star hacker on their side. At least a couple of good mercenaries, too, with an almost unlimited supply of weaponry. His agents had told them that in the car chase, they'd been fired at with a machine gun and had three different types of grenades thrown at them.

Strange. While the country had no shortage of mercenaries with access to illegal arms, Yuhle didn't have the money to hire them. As soon as Yuhle had gone into hiding, General Meade checked the scientist's bank account records. Yuhle had made a full withdrawal, not surprisingly, but the account hadn't had very much in it in the first place. An extensive trace turned up no other bank accounts for Yuhle in the United States or overseas. Yuhle didn't have enough money to stay on the run for more than a couple of months, and yet he had hired a crack team. Good mercenaries didn't come cheap.

Which could mean only two things— either he was getting financial backing from someone, or the members of his team were volunteers. The second possibility was the more disturbing one. Volunteers meant they couldn't be turned or bribed. It also meant they were probably out for him personally.

Assuming that, who would be out to get him? He'd made plenty of enemies in his career, but most were dead, in jail, or living overseas. That left a pretty short list, and some of those would stop short of taking on the US government. They had to be people with nothing to lose who had something against him or some strong motivation to help a people whom most of the world thought were simply a legend.

The general banged his fist on the desk. He was getting nowhere. He needed to find out more. He got up, went out of his office, and headed for the Poseidon Project laboratory.

He locked the office door behind him. As he passed through the front room, his assistant, Major Leticia Jefferson, stopped him. Half black and half Hispanic, Major Jefferson had gotten herself out of a terrible part of Spanish Harlem by volunteering for the army and earning a series of medals in war zones. She deserved a medal for all the indispensable help she'd been giving him on that project, but people didn't get medals for projects that didn't officially exist. It was one of the many unfair aspects of military life.

"I've printed out a few of the latest semi-declassified reports, sir," Major Jefferson said, handing over a manila envelope.

General Meade nodded in appreciation. The Pentagon was digitizing old reports from its archives. Many were still top secret but had become more accessible to him because they were on the army server. It saved him a trip through the vast military archives up in Washington, DC.

"What are they, Major?" he asked.

"What looks like an important report on the Roswell incident and a couple of brief reports on other sightings from the forties."

"Thank you, Major. Keep them until I return. By the way, please check on the location of every member of my blacklist. Check their recent movements for the past two months."

The blacklist had the names and details of Meade's enemies in the United States. If anyone could spot who might be helping Yuhle in his treachery, Major Jefferson could. She had a keen mind.

"Yes, sir."

General Meade turned and walked down the hallway then swiped his card through two different security doors to get to the laboratory of the Poseidon Project.

He entered a large room full of scientific equipment. Along one wall stood several man-sized cylindrical containers, looking a bit like upright coffins. A Plexiglas window on each of them showed the serene faces of several Atlanteans, held in a state of suspended animation until they were ready to be used. They reminded him of a rack of assault rifles, perfectly safe as long as they weren't touched, and deadly if they were taken down and put to use.

At least that was what he hoped they would be. Only one had been brought out of his unnatural slumber and put into the training program.

General Meade looked around the laboratory. No one else was there. Good. That meant Dr. Patrick Jones, his lead scientist, was actually working and not sneaking a look at Facebook. If Jones had had the work ethic of Dr. Yamazaki, the project would be ahead of schedule instead of barely keeping up.

He passed by a table filled with chemistry equipment, took a right around an electron microscope, and came to another door. Once again, he had to swipe his ID card through two sets of doors, his image being monitored by a series of cameras, before he emerged on a back lot.

The area was a few acres, surrounded by a sheer concrete wall thirty feet high and topped with razor wire. At each of the four corners, security cameras faced outward to search for intruders.

No camera faced inward. Even the security staff at the base weren't authorized to know what went on in that lot.

The area was broken up into several different types of terrain. From where General Meade stood, the ground went from flat gravel to a series of steep little hills. Out of sight to the right, he knew since he had designed the layout himself, stood a couple of small concrete buildings and some heaps of rubble. To his left, he could see the canopy of a lush bit of greenery planted to replicate jungle conditions.

It was a training ground to teach his Atlantean subject, Orion, how to fight in various environments. General Meade had modeled it on the training grounds he remembered as a cadet, with a few additions of his own. Beneath his feet ran a series of tunnels that were modeled after the sewers and steam tunnels that ran unseen, and mostly unknown, beneath all American towns and cities. Orion would get the best training General Meade could offer him in such a limited space.

Dr. Jones stood not far off, studying a tablet that showed all of Orion's vital signs. The scientist had put various monitors on the Atlantean and was studying how he reacted to stress and exertion.

General Meade was about to speak to the scientist when the crack of a rifle shot made him hurry forward. He didn't want to miss anything.

He scrambled over the series of steep, artificial hills, smiling as he noticed that despite being well into middle age, he could get up and down them without losing breath. He came to the summit of the last hillock, and from there, the general could see a series of low concrete buildings, typical of those in cities of the Middle East. A few large heaps of rubble lay here and there to add extra complexity to the terrain and to imitate the actual conditions of a heavily bombed city.

General Meade had fought in that sort of environment too many times. The High Command felt that the best way to pacify a city was to bomb it for weeks on end and then send in ground forces. What they didn't seem to understand was that if forces pounded on someone's neighborhood and killed a bunch of his friends and family without him having a chance to fight back, and then suddenly appeared on his street, he was not exactly going to come out of his bomb shelter with a smile on his face and an American flag in his hand. He would be looking for payback.

Unconsciously, the general rubbed and flexed his left shoulder, which was still a bit stiff and sore from an old wound.

He'd gotten a little payback himself in a place that looked much like that.

The rifle cracked again. Instinctively, General Meade ducked, even though he knew the shooter was firing only paint pellets. He located the shooter in a second, nestled in the shadow of a satellite dish on the rooftop. More men would be hidden inside the building.

General Meade scanned the area. The two best approaches to the building were the heap of rubble between him and it, and the drainage ditch flanked by shrubbery off to the left.

A flicker of movement in the ditch told him that Orion had taken the second option.

The sniper saw the movement too, and two shots kicked up dirt on either side of the ditch, leaving splotches of red paint on the ground.

Orion burst out of the ditch and, with incredible speed, sprinted for the heap of rubble. He moved so quickly that the sniper didn't have a chance to get a shot off until Orion was more than halfway to cover. Three shots plowed up the earth behind him as Orion ducked into a roll and went behind the nearest heap of broken concrete and rusted rebars. Orion was out of sight of the building and its occupants, while General Meade could still get a good look at him.

What a magnificent specimen! Orion could run faster than a gazelle and was stronger than a bear. He was getting clever too. Showing himself in that ditch had been a trick. He knew the sniper would be too slow to hit him before he ducked back down, and he made the sniper waste two rounds before Orion truly showed himself. That was why the guy didn't get off any more shots until Orion had almost gotten out of sight again.

Orion crouched behind the broken pile of concrete, planning his next move. The next obvious step was to dive to the right to a bigger pile of rubble slightly closer to the building. Of course the sniper would have the crosshairs of his rifle trained on the narrow gap between the two heaps of concrete, and even with Orion's speed, it would be tough to make it in time.

Orion sensed that too. He picked up a chunk of concrete the size of a dinner plate and, without showing himself to the shooters in the building, heaved it overhead. With uncanny accuracy, the piece of concrete sailed in a perfect arc to land on top of the roof. A cry from the rooftop told General Meade that Orion had made a hit.

General Meade rubbed his jaw. He hoped that man wasn't too badly injured. Orion got carried away sometimes, and one of the general's latest headaches was explaining to the Pentagon why soldiers under his command kept going to the hospital.

Orion was already on the move. He shot like a bullet to the next heap of rubble then disappeared around it to another bit of cover the general remembered was there. Eager to see the show, General Meade ran down to the rubble.

I wonder if I'll attract fire myself, he thought. *The men might want a bit of revenge for the tough training I'm putting them through.*

Just to be on the safe side, General Meade crouched low as he ran in a zigzag pattern. He followed Orion's lead, making the same moves he had in the approach to the enemy position. His body warmed up, and all the old wartime reflexes came back.

Feels good, he thought. *I've been behind my desk and in budget meetings for too long.*

A couple of more shots told him where Orion had disappeared. He had cut around to the side of the building and was trying to get inside.

General Meade sprinted between two piles of rubble. The ground behind him plumed up with a shot. He grinned. So, the boys were out to harass their commander, eh? He'd show them who was boss.

He hunkered behind the shelter of the concrete for a moment. Best be careful. Paint pellets wouldn't kill him, but they sure did hurt, and the paint took ages to get out of a uniform.

Another burst of fire from his forward right reminded him that he was missing the show. He zigzagged through the rubble and flattened himself against the wall of the nearest building. None of them could hit him unless they exposed themselves out a window, something every soldier was trained not to do.

A thud on the ground next to him made him look. He had just enough time to whip around the corner before the paint grenade went off, spraying the whole area with red dye. Not a drop hit him.

An open window pierced the wall just a few feet ahead. He heard a series of blows and the sound of falling bodies.

He took a quick peek through the window to check that there was no threat and then took a longer look. Three of his soldiers lay in a heap on the ground, and Orion was disappearing up a set of nearby stairs.

General Meade pulled himself through the window. He'd really have to talk to Orion about being gentler with the men. Gentleness didn't come naturally to him, though, and the whole point of the exercise was to turn him into a killing machine.

As the general passed by the groaning soldiers, he scooped up a gun, checked each way around the doorway, and headed up the stairs.

Silence.

He peered around the corner just in time to see Orion sneak into a room at the end of the hall. He moved as quietly as a cat, with a cat's natural grace and balance. The physical tests Dr. Jones had put him through had ranked him off the charts.

Between General Meade and Orion's position stood another doorway. A soldier snuck out of it, gun at the ready, following Orion.

General Meade shot him straight in the butt.

The soldier leaped and turned around, rubbing his rear end. He gave the general a confused look.

"You have to check both ways before coming into a hallway, soldier," General Meade said. "Every time."

The soldier's face fell with embarrassment. "Yes, sir."

Orion peeked out of the next room. "I was going to ambush him, sir."

General Meade chuckled and turned back to the soldier. "Looks like you got off easy then, private. He would have given you a harder lesson than I just did."

The soldier limped off, red paint dribbling down the back of his pants.

"Be careful, sir," Orion said. "This building isn't clear. I'm talking in order to make it more challenging. Now they know where I am."

General Meade nodded and ducked into the room where the soldier had been hiding. He heard a rush of air, and the next time he looked, Orion had disappeared.

A few seconds later, there was a brief cry. One more down.

General Meade snuck out again. No point in sitting around and missing all the fun.

He doubled back the way he had come, his rifle leveled, passing the stairwell and checking that the room beyond it was clear. Orion had gone the other way, so now he and his protégé were coming on the soldiers from both sides.

Just as the general was crossing the room, a soldier popped out from around the opposite doorway. The soldier and he fired simultaneously. General Meade heard the paint pellet whip close by his head while his own pellet splattered harmlessly on the doorframe.

General Meade scampered to the far wall, pressed himself close, and aimed for the doorway. The soldier would have to lean out in order to get a shot at him, unless he had...

A grenade rolled into the room. Firing at the doorway to cover his movement, the general leaped for the grenade and kicked it back through the doorway.

Then came a loud bang and an even louder curse. The soldier walked through the door, looking glum and dripping red paint from head to toe.

"You have to wait before you throw a grenade, private," General Meade told him. "I know it's the most unnatural thing in the world to hold a ticking bomb in your hand, but if you don't want it kicked back in your face, you need to learn to do that."

"Yes, sir," the private mumbled, heading down the hall and out of the combat zone.

Rapid firing from the adjoining room made the general hurry in that direction. He peered around a corner and found it was all over. A pair of soldiers lay on the floor, obviously roughed up, while Orion stood over them, his dark face beaming in triumph.

General Meade strolled into the room, a smile on his face. "You went easy on these two. They're still conscious."

Orion nodded to the general, turned, and was about to strike the nearest soldier.

"Stop!" General Meade shouted.

Orion stopped, his fist poised in the air, and looked at General Meade curiously.

"Well done, Orion. You won. Come with me."

The Atlantean scampered over like a puppy and bent to kiss the general's hand.

"Don't do that," General Meade snapped, pulling his hand away in disgust. The mind-control drugs Dr. Jones had given him, and the hypnotic treatment he'd undergone by a crackpot mesmerist, had turned Orion into not only a willing servant but also a slave. It went against everything General Meade believed in.

He didn't see a way around it, though. The Poseidon Project needed a success story to keep its funding from being canceled, and the government needed a trained killer to go after Yuhle's team and that group of rogue Atlanteans. Beyond that, Orion was far more important as the first recruit for a new army of super soldiers who were Earth's only hope against an alien invasion.

"You're getting better and better, Orion."

"I train every day, master."

"Call me general, or sir. I don't like it when you call me master."

"I'm very sorry, master."

General Meade ground his teeth. With all that mental conditioning, there were some things that couldn't be helped. What would his proud forefathers who helped free the slaves during the Civil War think if they could see him one hundred fifty years later, having created his own slave?

He pushed his guilt aside. More important things were at stake.

"I'm going to send you on a mission soon, Orion."

"Whatever my master wishes."

"You'll have to kill some people, perhaps many people. Will you be able to do that?"

"I will do whatever my master wishes."

"That's what I was afraid of," General Meade mumbled. He looked around at the bleak concrete building and the ruins outside the window and remembered his many tours of duty. Things had been clearer then. It was kill or be killed. Simple. No second thoughts.

The people he was up against weren't bad people, they weren't gangsters or extremists, but they were in the way. They could do far more damage to the world than the Mob or the Islamists or the Cocaine Cartel or any of them. The future of the whole world hung in the balance. The Atlanteans needed to be forced to obey, and Dr. Yuhle and his group needed to be wiped out.

It needed to be done fast, and it needed to be done right.

"You know, Orion, I think I just might be going with you. It will be nice to get rid of these troublemakers personally."

Chapter 6

JUNE 19, 2016, THE DESERT JUST
OUTSIDE YUMA, ARIZONA

7:10 AM

If Otto had been tired before, he was by then half dead with exhaustion. The light of a harsh desert morning jabbed into his gritty eyes as Vivian drove the car through southwestern Arizona. Yuhle lay snoring in the passenger's seat, his endurance having given out hours before, and Dr. Yamazaki was curled up on the backseat, taking up most of the space and forcing Otto to squeeze up against the door.

The desert there was different. In New Mexico and Nevada, it was greener, with bushes and cacti and the occasional tree. When they had passed through the Sonora Desert near Tucson the night before, he'd seen towering saguaro cacti silhouetted against the starry vault of the sky, with the Milky Way arcing high overhead. It had made a beautiful, eerie backdrop to his fitful sleep.

Through the night, they had headed south, until dawn found them in a barren landscape. The low tan humps of sand dunes stretched as far as the eye could see, looking like the backs of half-buried camels. Not a tree or cactus was in sight. Nothing green, no color at all except for the pale brown of the land and the washed-out blue of the sky. Despite it being early, he could feel the heat pushing through the glass of the window.

They'd taken the back roads and stayed out of sight, hoping they wouldn't come across a patrol car and have to explain the bullet holes in their windows and the shattered taillight and side view mirror. They had no explanation handy, and Otto didn't want to know what Vivian would do to any cop unlucky enough to stop them.

Otto had snatched only an hour or two of restless sleep the night before, and those hours had been filled with terrible, majestic dreams of fire and burning. He awoke feeling sick, sick at himself and sick at the helpless, terrifying situation he had found himself in. When the Atlantis Allegiance broke him out of jail, he had followed them on impulse, both to get free of the chain gang and to help Jaxon.

But clearly he was in another prison, another chain gang, and every minute put another mile between him and his girlfriend.

It was strange to think how attached he had become to her, even though they had spent only a couple of weeks together. She was something special. He could tell that even before he learned about her powers and her strange heritage. No way would he leave her in the clutches of someone like General Meade. His men had tried to kill them the day before, and as useful as Jaxon was to the Poseidon Project, Otto had no doubt the general would kill her without a second thought if she caused him trouble.

But how could he and the rest of the Atlantis Allegiance save her? They were having trouble enough saving themselves.

Otto noticed Vivian checking a map. She'd turned off the GPS and all the phones in the car, saying their signals could be tracked, and was relying on an old road map like his parents used before everyone got smartphones.

A mile marker flicked by. Vivian turned her head to read it and then drove another half mile or so, slowing down all the while.

Otto spotted a faint dirt track heading off through the desert. It was flatter there, and the track led almost invisibly to a line of low, stony hills in the distance. He noticed fresh tracks of several vehicles along the trail as they pulled in and followed it. Not too long ago, he wouldn't have noticed a detail like that. Today his eyes were wide open. He felt that before he had joined the Atlantis Allegiance, he had been sleepwalking through life.

Sleep. When would he get some more? When would he get a chance to rest? Perhaps in whatever godforsaken hideout that gorgeous mercenary was taking him to next. Grunt and Edward were probably already there. They had been able to take a more direct route along the interstate and state highways and not slink along half-forgotten county roads for several hundred miles.

They approached the hills. Vivian flicked the headlights on and off three times.

"Someone watching us?" Otto asked, keeping his voice to a whisper so as not to wake up the others.

"Grunt or one of his buddies will be up there with a sniper's rifle, covering the approach. His buddies are kind of jumpy."

"Who are they?"

"Tohono O'odham."

"What's that?"

"It's a Native American tribe. Their traditional lands straddle the US-Mexico border, and they have contacts on either side. Actually, their stomping grounds are to the east, just south of Tucson and all the way to Nogales on the border, but these particular Tohono O'odham like a bit more privacy."

"Were they exiled from their tribe?" Otto asked.

Vivian looked at him through the rearview mirror, one eyebrow raised. "You're a suspicious young man, aren't you?"

"I've been hanging out with you guys too long."

Vivian grinned. "I don't know the answer to your question, but I can guess. Oh, and you probably shouldn't ask them. They make Grunt look like a kitten."

"Ah…right."

As the car passed through a gap in the hills, Vivian leaned forward and waved to the top of the nearest summit. Otto craned his neck but couldn't see anyone up there. Briefly, he wondered if he was in the crosshairs of Grunt's rifle and was surprised to realize that thought didn't bother him anymore. He'd been through too much in the past few months to be bothered by anything short of a gunfight.

The track meandered between several hills and dipped down into a small valley. At the bottom, Otto spotted the trailers that had made up the Atlantis Allegiance base near the Nevada Test Site. Next to them were parked Grunt's Hummer and several battered old pickup trucks.

Movement off to his right caught his eye. A brown-skinned man wearing jeans, a checked shirt, and a cowboy hat waved a rifle over his head from the nearest hilltop.

"Wake up, sleepyheads!" Vivian called out. "End of the line. Again. Why can't we hide out in Vegas or New York City or someplace fun?"

Dr. Yamazaki stirred and rubbed her eyes. Yuhle continued snoring.

Vivian steered the Subaru down a rocky slope, the car's undercarriage scraping stone. Even that noise didn't wake Yuhle.

"We're lucky we haven't popped a tire with all this off-roading we've been doing," Otto said.

"Special tires," Vivian said. "You can shoot them, and they won't go flat. All our vehicles have them, of course."

"Of course," Otto muttered, shaking his head. He'd fended off an attack by government agents, and he still felt way out of his depth.

As Vivian parked next to the trailers, several Native American men and women gathered around. All of them carried hunting rifles and had pistols holstered at their hips. They stared at the vehicle, their expressions stony and unreadable.

Otto stepped out of the car and smiled at them uncertainly. One man stepped forward. He was shorter than Otto but twice as wide. The rifle in his hand wasn't nearly as scary as the scowl on his face. Otto's heart did a flip-flop when he saw the man was wearing a dark-blue baseball cap reading "FBI."

Otto stopped short.

"Jim Running Horse, special agent with the FBI," the man said. "I've heard someone has been setting fires around here. You wouldn't know anything about that, would you?"

A second Native American came up behind him. He, too, wore an FBI cap and was much bigger than the first man, with a huge belly and arms the size of tree trunks.

"I-I didn't set any fires," Otto said, looking back and forth between the two.

"We have it on good authority that you're a pyromaniac. Do you deny it?" the big one said.

Otto groaned and rolled his eyes. "Very funny. Grunt put you up to this, didn't he? You're not FBI."

"Not FBI!" the little one shouted, making Otto jump. "Do you even know what FBI stands for?"

"Ah...Federal Bureau of Investigation?"

The small one made a clucking noise, as though Otto had said something stupid. He looked back at the others, who shook their heads, then took a step forward.

"No, it stands for Fry Bread Inspector."

Otto stared at him.

The giant behind him added, "Or Freaking Big Indian!"

All the Tohono O'odham broke out in laughter. Otto felt himself turn red.

The whine of a dirt bike made them turn. Grunt came riding down the side of the nearest hill at breakneck speed. He had a rifle strapped to his broad back and, as usual, was dressed in full camo that could barely contain the muscles that threatened to burst out of the material. The tribal tattoo on his shaven head was clearly visible even from a distance.

Grunt skidded to a stop inches from Otto, eliciting another flinch from him and more laughter from the Tohono O'odham.

"Hey, Pyro! How's it hanging?"

"Nice to see you, Grunt. We're still alive, as you can see."

Grunt glanced at the car, where Dr. Yamazaki and a sleepy-eyed Yuhle were just getting out.

"What do you think of her?" Grunt asked in a low voice.

"Not sure, but I think she's okay. If she was trying to con us, she would have made up a better story and hidden the tracking device better."

Grunt thought for a moment before saying, "Well, it looks like we're stuck with her now. Keep an eye on her, will you?"

Otto nodded. "So now what?"

Vivian came up to them. "Dunno. First we have to make sure we really got away. Now that we have both scientists, that changes things. If she turns out all right, Dr. Yamazaki will be a big help to us. And that group of Atlanteans that supposedly helped her would make good allies."

Otto noticed that Yuhle and Dr. Yamazaki were talking a little distance apart, casting nervous glances at the rest of them. The Tohono O'odham lounged about nearby, watching, their guns in their hands.

"But we don't know how to get in touch with them," Otto said. "We didn't even know they existed until yesterday."

"Yeah, but it seems like they know we exist, Pyro, or at least they knew all about where the doc was laid up," Grunt replied. "We need to see what Edward thinks."

"Where is Edward, anyway? Hiding in his trailer as usual?" Otto asked.

Grunt jerked a thumb in the direction of the largest of the three trailers. A tall aerial and satellite dish took up much of the roof. "Yup. He's got some interesting stuff to tell us, so let's get going."

They headed over to the trailer, Yuhle and Dr. Yamazaki following a little distance behind. Before they had made it ten feet, Edward came bursting out of the door, waving his arms.

"Don't bring her close! Keep her away!"

Everyone stopped. Otto heard some of the Tohono O'odham chuckling behind him.

Edward was an overweight man in his twenties, pale and out of shape from spending all his time in front of the computer. He wore baggy jeans and a stained T-shirt. His belly bulged out between them. Edward blinked at the bright sunlight for a moment and then hurried back into the trailer.

He appeared again a few seconds later, holding an oblong black box with a couple of buttons and dials on it. Shading his eyes from the sun, he walked over to Dr. Yamazaki.

"They already searched me," Dr. Yamazaki protested.

"And I'm going to search you again," Edward grumbled.

He flicked on the device and made a slow pass from the scientist's head to her feet, then did the same with Yuhle, who looked confused. Once he was finished, he went over to Vivian and Otto and made passes over them too.

"You need to relax, Edward. Why would we have a tracking device?" Otto said, laughing.

"Hey, Pyro! Glad to see you survived. She might have planted one on you, ever thought of that?" Edward said. "Hmmm, negative on all of you. Better check the car."

Edward wandered over to the Subaru and started to scan it. Jim Running Horse, the short Tohono O'odham who had been teasing Otto before, and who looked to be the leader, went over to Grunt and started speaking to him in Spanish. Otto was impressed to hear Grunt reply fluently. When he had first met him, Otto had figured Grunt was just a mindless killing machine, but every once in a while, he showed something deeper. Otto joined them.

"So, um, how do you guys fit in?"

Jim Running Horse looked him up and down. "Grunt and I were in the war together."

"Which war?"

Jim Running Horse spoke to Grunt in Spanish, and they both laughed.

Otto blushed again. Why was he always the butt of jokes with Grunt? He turned to the mercenary.

"So, um, how much do they know?"

"About the Atlanteans?" Jim Running Horse asked, giving him a direct gaze. "We've known about them a couple of thousand years longer than you have, buddy."

"Do you know where we can find them?" Otto asked.

"Ha!" Jim Running Horse nudged Grunt, who grinned back at him. "This guy's a comedian."

Edward finished his scan of the car and everyone who had been on the Albuquerque mission and said, "Okay, folks, why don't you come on into my office? I have some things to show you."

As everyone moved to follow, Edward turned to Dr. Yamazaki. "And where do you think you're going?"

Dr. Yamazaki blushed and walked away.

"Don't be too hard on her," Otto said.

"She could be one of them."

"More likely she's one of us. Let's not split the group over this, huh?"

Edward shrugged and headed for his trailer. The Atlantis Allegiance, plus Jim Running Horse, followed. Even Yuhle, after pausing and looking at his former boss, went along.

The interior of Edward's trailer hadn't changed when he picked up stakes and moved to a new spot in the middle of an empty desert. The windows were still covered with black cloth, and the only light came from three computer screens on a desk. The rest of the trailer was filled with gadgets and spare electronic parts Otto couldn't identify. Behind Edward's desk stood another, smaller desk on which a shortwave radio played.

"Seven...twelve...twenty-nine...five..." a female announcer said over the hiss of static. Even though she spoke in English, she had an accent. It sounded Slavic, Russian maybe.

Otto wrinkled his nose. Yeah, pretty much the same, right down to the smell of old socks, rotting junk food, and Edward's unwashed body.

Edward sat down at his desk, the three computers and their three keyboards arranged around him. He pushed aside an empty potato chip bag, started tapping away at the keyboard, and brought up several files in rapid succession. The Slavic woman droned in the background, reciting a seemingly pointless series of numbers.

Otto and the others stood behind him, watching. Soon all three screens were filled with images of UFOs, one of Edward's many strange obsessions. Although most of the images were the usual blurry shots, some were startlingly clear. Many of the images seemed to be of the typical disk-shaped UFOs, the old-style "flying saucers," while others were cigar-shaped, and one computer showed a brief film clip of what looked like a glowing amoeba passing in front of some Northern Lights.

The photo of one disk caught Otto's eye. It had been taken from above, the east coast of North America clearly visible far below. Edward pointed at that image.

"Look familiar?" Edward asked.

Nobody answered.

Edward raised his hands in the air in frustration. "Anyone hear of Roswell?"

"That's where a UFO crashed in New Mexico, right?" Otto said.

"Yeah," Edward said, nodding. "It's the most famous crash site, but it sure isn't the only one. This disk is an exact match of the craft that crashed at Roswell in 1947. I have the secret Roswell files right here."

He punched a few keys on the keyboard and brought up some fuzzy scans of old documents. Several black-and-white photographs showed a disk-shaped craft broken up in a field, only the back half remaining in one piece. Edward scrolled down to images of various parts of the debris.

"I haven't seen these photos before," Jim Running Horse said. "I thought I had all the files."

"I just cracked this a week ago. The Pentagon only recently put this report on their server. They've been scanning a lot of old documents lately. I'll send it to your Tor account," Edward said.

"Tor isn't invulnerable," the Tohono O'odham said. "Give it to me on a memory stick. If General Meade is that careful, then I'm going to be that careful too."

"Smart man," Edward said with a nod as he continued to scroll down. Otto sensed Edward had been testing him.

Otto looked from the Native American to the computer hacker and back again. Once more, he felt as though he was being left out.

Edward stopped scrolling and zoomed in on a small strip of material, its edge jagged from where it had been torn from a larger piece. Strange markings were on it, a series of lines and dots that almost looked like writing. Soon Otto saw a pattern of four different symbols—a short line, a long line, a single dot, and a double dot.

Jim Running Horse leaned in and took a closer look. "This is different from the other script."

"What other script?" Otto asked.

"Several pieces like this were found at the Roswell crash," the Tohono O'odham replied. "They had writing on them. Linguistic experts have been trying to decipher them ever since, but it's a hard job because there isn't enough material to make the usual comparisons. I've stared at the stuff myself for years and can't make head or tail of it. This sample, though, is totally different from the other texts I've seen."

Otto looked Jim Running Horse up and down. Dusty boots, worn-out jeans, a checked shirt, the deep-brown, wrinkled face of someone who had spent a lifetime working outside, and a battered but clean old rifle. The guy looked like a rancher and talked like a professor.

"Who are you?" Otto asked.

Jim Running Horse's face didn't change. "I'm Jim Running Horse, I told you."

Otto shook his head and turned back to Edward. "So is this script the piece of the puzzle you need to decipher the alien language?"

The fact that he asked that question in all seriousness and expected a believable answer told Otto that he had positively, definitely been hanging out with those people too long.

Suddenly, Yuhle shouldered him aside and stared at the screen, his mouth hanging open. Edward looked at the scientist and smiled.

"Not exactly," the computer hacker said.

He punched another key, and a genetic sequence came up on the screen.

"There," Yuhle said, pointing at one part of the double helix.

"Right you are," Edward said, tapping away at his keyboard.

The screen zoomed in on the part of the DNA sequence Yuhle had indicated and then cut it into a separate image. As Edward worked, Yuhle adjusted his glasses and explained.

"As some of you may know, most of the genetic sequence for any animal has things in common with other animals. We are all descended from the same proto-plasmic organism billions of years ago, and things like mammals or primates are a blink in the eye in the time of evolution, so it's not surprising that, for example, a chimpanzee and a human share 96 percent of the same genes. Not only that, but their DNA is made up of the same four building blocks—adenine, thymine, guanine, and cytosine. You can see them marked here on the computer as A, T, G, and C. It's the same with the Atlantis gene and human genes. Atlanteans are almost entirely human, their genetic code almost indistinguishable from that of an ordinary human being.

"Almost, but not quite. They have a few extra sequences, still with the same four building blocks you find in all genomes, and these sequences are what we call the Atlantis genes. There aren't very many of them, and I've been studying them so intensely that I know them by sight. The one I pointed out is one of them, but I never thought Edward was going to show it to me in this context."

Edward took the cue and brought up the image of the strip of alien material with the markings on it. He overlaid the image of the Atlantis genes on it.

They made a perfect match. Each of the four different types of gene building blocks matched up with a different symbol on the piece of alien craft from Roswell.

Everyone stared in silence for a minute. Edward chuckled.

"No prize for guessing the significance of this," he said.

Otto shook his head in wonder. "Edward, I never thought I'd say this, but you've turned me into a conspiracy theorist."

Chapter 7

JUNE 19, 2016, LOS ANGELES,
CALIFORNIA

7:10 AM

"You're getting much better," said Jaxon's martial arts instructor, Marquis. "You're much more focused than you used to be."

"I figured out this stuff might come in handy someday," Jaxon replied.

They faced off in the exercise room of the Grants' home. As usual, Marquis had laid down mats on the floor, and the two were dressed in traditional aikido training uniforms—a white cotton top similar to ones used in karate classes, and a pair of pleated black cotton pants.

"Let's try another move," Marquis said.

He showed her how someone might grab her around the neck from behind and demonstrated how to put that person off balance, flip them, and strike them with her foot. Then it was Jaxon's turn, and she executed the move perfectly.

"Well done!" Marquis said as he got up from the mat.

Out of the corner of her eye, Jaxon saw Isadore standing in the doorway, nodding. Her foster mother took a close interest in her martial arts education. Jaxon wasn't sure why. She'd given up trying to figure out Stephen and Isadore.

"Let's do it again," Marquis said. "My own teacher once said that you don't truly know a move until you've practiced it a thousand times."

"Then this is going to be a long class," Jaxon said with a smile.

"Your whole life is a class," Marquis said. Without warning, he grabbed her from behind, putting an arm around her throat. She twisted, knocked his feet out from under him, and flipped him over her body.

Marquis landed on the mat with a thump.

"Well done again!"

"Only nine hundred ninety-eight more to go," Jaxon said.

They continued to practice, Jaxon asking the occasional question and Marquis showing her more techniques, while Isadore watched, silent, through the entire class.

Despite having spent most of the night wandering around Los Angeles, Jaxon didn't feel at all tired. She wondered if superhuman endurance was another of her powers or if the rush of finally doing something interesting had given her a day's worth of adrenaline.

She couldn't believe she had gotten away with it. Grant and Isadore hadn't heard her leap out of her window, had slept through her entire absence, and hadn't even woken up during her noisy climb up the drainpipe and back through her bedroom window.

Jaxon had wandered around unfamiliar neighborhoods for several hours, strolling down dark, lonely residential streets and along a blaring highway. Nothing much had happened, but the thrill of being out and free had lifted her spirits. She hated being forced into someone else's mold. Some foster parent or counselor or group home director was always telling her how to behave and trying to make her into what they wanted her to be. Just sneaking out for a walk was an act of rebellion, and it made her feel great.

Of course it was insane for a sixteen-year-old girl to walk alone through LA at night, but she was no ordinary sixteen-year-old girl. To her surprise, she wasn't attacked. A couple of times, guys shouted from passing cars, and a police car had slowed down across the street from her, forcing her to duck out of sight down an alley, but otherwise, she was left alone.

She felt strangely disappointed at that, as though she had wanted to get into a fight. She'd been holding in her emotions for so long, resisting the urge to knock out bullies like Courtney, she would have invited the excuse to lay some pervert flat out on the pavement.

"Okay, Jaxon," Isadore finally said as Marquis was showing her another technique. "It's time to get ready for school."

No sweat, Jaxon thought. *If I can handle walking alone at night, I can handle that too.*

She reminded herself to be careful. Someone out there was looking for her, hunting her, and she didn't know why. They had found out about her powers somehow, and she had to lie low. Getting away from their notice was the whole reason she wanted to leave the group home in the first place. She could enjoy her moonlit walks, but she still needed to play the part of the good little girl at home and school.

She went through her day in a haze, ignoring the taunts of Courtney and her crew, struggling with her coursework as usual, and all the while waiting for sunset so she could go out and explore some more.

Jaxon didn't get her chance until late in the night. While Isadore had gone to bed at her usual early hour, Stephen had stayed up late to work in the greenhouse. Jaxon had pretended to go to bed too and kept her light off as she waited for him to turn in. After an hour, she grew impatient and parted her curtain a little to watch him. It was hard to see through all the greenery, but she could tell Stephen was bustling around the greenhouse with a notepad in his hand, writing furiously. He kept going over to the spot where Jaxon had planted her vegetables.

She frowned. What could he want with those? They weren't part of his experiments. He worked on plant toxins. Jaxon's vegetables were the only plants in the whole greenhouse that couldn't kill you.

At last, Stephen turned off the light, and Jaxon heard him come inside, go upstairs, and go to bed. Jaxon decided to wait half an hour to make sure he was asleep before sneaking out.

In the meantime, she decided to try a little experiment of her own. A few days ago, she had been reaching for something, and it had leaped into her hand without her having to touch it. That had scared her to death, and she hadn't tried it again. It was even stranger than her ability to make plants grow.

Her heart beating fast, she sat down at her desk. She parted the curtains a little again so the light from the moon and the city dimly illuminated her room. All was quiet. Her desk was tidy and organized as her foster parents insisted, textbooks to one side, notebooks to the other, and a pen sitting in between.

She opened her hand and held it close to the pen. Focusing her mind, she tensed her hand and willed the pen to come to her. It didn't move.

Frowning, she tried again, harder that time, her hand straining. Nothing happened.

"This worked before," Jaxon muttered. "Why isn't it working now?"

What was it Juliette, her yoga and meditation instructor, had said? You had to empty your mind. Some religion called Taoism said that not trying often produced more results than trying. Juliette had given the example of water running over a stone. Water was soft, but over time it would wear a stone smooth and eventually wear it away entirely.

Juliette had given her that lesson as life advice, hinting that too often, Jaxon flailed away at her problems, trying to solve them through brute force before quickly giving up in frustration. The better way, Juliette had suggested, was to work at them softly, persistently.

Jaxon chuckled. It was as if Juliette had access to every therapist's report that had ever been written about her.

She held out her hand, trying to relax her muscles and empty her mind. She closed her hand as though she was going to pick up the pen the normal way. That was what had happened when she had moved an object by accident the first time. She had reached for it, and it had come to her.

But she hadn't even been trying to move the object. And why hadn't it happened by accident since then? How could she control that power if it happened only when it felt like it?

She tried again, holding her hand for a full five minutes and feeling a little foolish. She put her hand on her lap then brought it back up again. That didn't work either.

Jaxon bit her lip. What should she try next?

She brought her finger down next to the tip of the pen and pushed it in a circle, moving it around and around like a propeller. That was getting boring. What was the point of having a power if she couldn't turn it on or off? She couldn't make that work, and she couldn't turn off her ability to grow plants. She had to wear double gloves in order to touch seeds without them sprouting.

She was missing something. Both of those powers had come about only recently, unlike her strength, which had manifested at age nine. Did the powers develop as the body developed? Was that part of her growing up? Maybe she'd develop even more of them.

Or perhaps they developed as she needed them. She was still a kid when she first showed her strength, and that had been to stop a grown man from messing with her. Perhaps those powers were a response to danger too. But what danger? The plant thing had come around well before those guys attacked her in the greenhouse, and she wasn't in danger at the moment.

Jaxon stared out the window, absent-mindedly spinning the pen in circles. She saw no point in developing more of those weird abilities if she couldn't control them. They'd only make her life even more complicated than it already was.

She took her finger away from the pen to scratch her ear. A sound from the desk made her look down.

The pen was still spinning.

Jaxon blinked. Okay, maybe it would still spin for a second or two, but it hadn't even slowed down.

Jaxon brought her finger to just above the pen and started twirling it around without touching the pen. The pen's movement sped up. She spun her finger in the other direction. The pen stopped and started spinning in the same direction as her finger.

She cupped her hand as though she was going to pick the pen up, and it flew into her grasp. Startled, she dropped the pen, then reached out again.

It flew into her hand a second time.

She carefully put the pen down and tried to move it again. That time, it didn't budge.

Jaxon's brow furrowed. What was wrong? She kept trying and found her power had left her again.

Perhaps it's only developing just now, kind of like a baby learning to walk, Jaxon thought. *A baby keeps falling down until it learns what to do. The pen started moving when I was distracted, so Juliette was right about that. Trying to force something isn't the right way.*

She chuckled. If only she could convince the bullies, foster parents, teachers, and counselors of that philosophy.

Jaxon stood, deciding to work on it more tomorrow. Right then, the city beckoned. She wanted to get out there and explore. It was the only freedom she had.

It took her only a moment to get out the window and jump to the ground. As with the previous time, she landed without hurting herself.

Putting her hood up, she looked around, wondering where to go. She'd gone out back before, cutting across a residential area before making it to the highway. That night, she'd explore somewhere different.

She circled the house, instinctively staying close to the wall so that if Grant or Isadore happened to look out an upstairs window, they wouldn't see her, and she cut across the front lawn. The neighborhood was a bit of a mystery to her. The Grants never spoke to the neighbors, and no one ever walked along the perfectly kept sidewalk that ran along one side of the street. It was a cul-de-sac and had hardly any traffic, even during the day. But at the moment, it was abandoned, and the only sounds she could hear besides the distant rush of the city all around were the chirping of crickets.

The houses in that area were big, some even bigger than the Grants' place. All were set back from the road, behind fences and broad lawns. Some were hidden behind a screen of hedges or trees. No lights shone except for the occasional front porch light left on and one or two upstairs lights. It was a strange feeling to be in so much darkness and isolation in the middle of a huge, sprawling city.

Jaxon strolled down the sidewalk, hands in her pockets, enjoying the isolation and quiet. Too bad the Grants didn't have a country home. That would be even better. She had lived in cities all her life and enjoyed the fun they had to offer, but if she was going to be cut off from the world as the Grants wanted her to be, it would be nice to enjoy some nature and quiet.

A few bright stars twinkled through the haze. Jaxon smiled. Not many neighborhoods in Los Angeles where residents could see stars at night.

But that neighborhood was too peaceful, too respectable. She was never going to find any excitement there.

A noise up ahead told her she was wrong.

She heard a muffled cry, mocking laughter, and the scuff of a shoe on pavement. Curious, she picked up her pace.

Coming around a bend in the road, she saw three figures struggling by the sidewalk next to a parked car. The car's door was open, and light from inside illuminated the scene. Two well-dressed middle-aged men, one with a big paunch and the other bald except for a thin fringe of hair around the sides and back, were struggling with a young woman dressed in a short leather skirt, halter top, and high heels.

Jaxon stopped. She stood within the shadow of a tree and knew that with them standing next to the light, it would be hard for them to spot her. She watched, unsure, and with a pounding heart tried to figure out exactly what was happening.

The car was obviously the woman's, a beat-up old Nissan that looked ten years old. Baldy and Paunchy looked too well off to be driving something like that. In fact, Jaxon thought she recognized Baldy. Hadn't she seen him drive past on that very same street? That was probably his house they were struggling in front of.

"Give me what you owe me!" the woman said.

"Come on baby, one for the road?" Paunchy said as Baldy giggled.

Each of them had grabbed one of her arms, and they were pulling her back and forth as she tried to break free. Even with two against one, the woman was holding her own.

"Let's take her back to the house," Baldy said, giggling again.

"You want extra, you got to pay for extra, and you got to pay for what you already had."

"We're going to get extra and not pay you at all, you cheap bit of tail," Paunchy said.

Jaxon tensed. A prostitute and two rough customers.

The two men, both old enough to be the prostitute's father, started dragging her across the lawn and back to the house.

Rage rose up within Jaxon. She remembered her foster father, Mr. Spencer, the one whose wrist she had to break to keep him from touching her. She remembered the rude calls from the men driving past the previous night. She remembered all the unwelcome looks and jokes and hints from all the pushy guys she'd ever met.

Making sure her hood was up and that it obscured her features, she strode across the lawn.

Baldy saw her first. He stared at her for a moment, half frightened at being discovered and half annoyed to have someone interrupt his fun, and then he called out in a snide voice, "Hey, girl, you want to join the party?"

Paunchy snickered. Jaxon guessed both were drunk.

"Let her go," Jaxon demanded, still approaching them.

The prostitute took one look at her and shouted, "Kid, get out of here. They'll hurt you!"

Baldy giggled again—*What is it with the giggles?* Jaxon wondered—and then said, "Hurt you? Oh no, we won't hurt you. Come on inside. You're going to like this."

With that, he pushed the prostitute into Paunchy's arms and walked toward Jaxon, leering.

Jaxon took a final two steps and slugged him.

In her rage, she forgot to hold back, perhaps never even wanted to. She was beyond thinking, she was only feeling, and her feelings went from anger to shock as she saw Baldy spin around like a top, blood spurting from his mouth, and collapse at her feet.

He lay there, moaning, his jaw set at an unnatural angle.

Jaxon froze, completely stunned. Had she done that?

"Jesus Christ!" Paunchy cried, letting go of the prostitute. He fumbled in his pocket and pulled out a clasp knife. The prostitute backed away as the light from the car gleamed on four inches of sharp steel.

The sight snapped Jaxon out of it. Marquis had trained her in a couple of techniques to use on a knife-wielding opponent.

Stopping him proved ridiculously easy. Paunchy came at her in a clumsy fashion, waving the blade back and forth and obviously thinking that a teenage girl would squeal and plead for mercy at the sight of a knife. It hadn't gotten through his alcoholic haze that she had just flattened his friend and wasn't retreating an inch.

As he got within reach, Jaxon grabbed his wrist with her right hand and pressed her left forearm against his elbow. The pressure kept him from moving his arm, and she didn't even need to use her extra strength to bring him down to the ground. He ended up flat on his face, with his arm still pinioned between her knee and her forearm as she knelt beside him.

"Let me go!" he squawked.

"Quiet," Jaxon growled, looking around to make sure they weren't being watched. The prostitute had recovered quickly. She had gone over to where Baldy lay groaning and bleeding on the ground, pulled his wallet out of his pocket, and removed the money.

"Payment in full," she grumbled, tossing the wallet at him.

She strolled over to Jaxon.

"Thanks, girl. What are you going to do with this guy?" she asked.

Jaxon looked from him to her and back again.

"Depends. What were they going to do to you?"

"Come on. You ain't that young. What do you think? The reason I left was because after the usual stuff, they wanted some things that even I don't do. Turns out, they didn't want to take no for an answer."

"Things? What things?"

"Nothing you need to know about, girl," the prostitute said, her voice laden with disgust.

Jaxon scowled at the helpless man on the ground. What would disgust a prostitute? She decided she didn't want to try to figure that out.

With a snarl, she pressed down on his elbow and heard it snap. Paunchy wailed in pain.

Jaxon stood up, feeling lightheaded.

"You better go," Jaxon told the woman.

A light came on in the house across the street.

"You too," the woman said. "And thanks."

They hurried across the lawn together, Jaxon headed for home and the prostitute headed for her car.

"What's your name?" Jaxon asked.

"Candy."

"No, I mean your real name."

"Melissa, not that anyone ever cared. They started calling me Candy at the group home."

Something in Jaxon's stomach turned and went cold.

"What's your name?" the prostitute asked.

Jaxon paused. "Malkia."

"Cool name. What does it mean?"

"It's Swahili for 'queen.'"

The prostitute smiled. "Cool."

A black girl at one of her old group homes had taught it to her. For some reason, Jaxon felt it fit.

"Take care of yourself," Jaxon told her. With that, Jaxon turned away and disappeared into the darkness.

Chapter 8

JUNE 19, 2016, THE DESERT JUST
OUTSIDE YUMA, ARIZONA

8:30 PM

Otto and the others sat around a large campfire at the center of the parked vehicles. Rocks and a couple of coolers served as seats. A few of the Tohono O'odham were on sentry duty up on the hilltops, but otherwise everyone had assembled for a big meeting. After much discussion and debate, Dr. Yamazaki had been allowed to attend too.

A couple of the Tohono O'odham were roasting rabbits on a spit over the fire, while someone else had placed a grill over some of the coals and was cooking up a bunch of steaks that he had pulled from a cooler in the back of one of the pickups. Dozens of potatoes wrapped in aluminum foil roasted in the coals. Cans of beer and soda were making the rounds. If it hadn't been for all the guns and secrecy, Otto would have felt as though he was on a big camping trip.

Even though they shared the same circle with the Atlantis Allegiance, the Tohono O'odham kept to themselves, speaking their own language. It was a strange, halting tongue, with a lot of Spanish words in it. That part of the country had been colonized by the Spanish five hundred years ago, and the old language had made it into every culture in the land.

Jim Running Horse stood up and addressed the crowd first. Otto noticed that he hadn't put away his firearm. None of the Tohono O'odham had. Neither had Grunt or Vivian, for that matter.

"Now some of you I've known for a long time"—Jim Running Horse nodded at Grunt and then glanced at the rest of the Atlantis Allegiance—"and some of you are new to me. I just want you to know that all my people here today can be trusted. We've been through too much for too long ever to sell you out to the Feds. Hell, I wouldn't sell my worst enemy to the white government, and you sure aren't my worst enemies. Anything said here tonight will stay within this group. You have my word on that."

Jim Running Horse sat down.

Grunt nodded and replied, "I know your people can be trusted, Jim, and I've relied on that trust several times. Any friend of yours is a friend of mine. As for the newbies, well, they'll get to know you in time, and in the meantime, they're just going to have to trust my judgment. First order of business is to bring our two groups up to speed. I know just enough T.O. to know you guys have been talking about us ever since we got here"—that elicited a grin from Jim Running Horse—"so there's no need for introductions. As you know, we saved Dr. Yamazaki here from the clutches of General Meade. I already told you all her story, and she herself knows a lot of us have problems believing it, but she needs to be here tonight because she knows more about the Atlantis gene than anyone."

Grunt turned to the others in the Atlantis Allegiance. The firelight made his tribal tattoo stand out as deep black against his reddened scalp. His face was set with a deadly seriousness, so different from his usual joking, cynical demeanor.

"Now you're probably wondering about all these grim-faced guys and gals packing weaponry and camping out in the middle of the ugliest desert in America. They're a group of Tohono O'odham that split off from their tribe because the Tribal Council was doing things they didn't agree with. These folks are traditionalists and don't like how the Tribal Council allows casinos on their land and turns a blind eye to mining and liquor dealing. They see the Tribal Council as puppets of the US government, and considering some of the decisions the council makes, it's hard to blame them for thinking that. This is only one branch of this group. Other tribes have their own traditionalists fighting to preserve their ways, and they're all in contact with one another."

Yuhle raised an uncertain hand, as though he was a nervous student asking a question in class. "So what's the name of this organization?"

Jim Running Horse shrugged. "No name. Just decent people getting together to do what's right."

Otto wondered if that was true. A nationwide organization that didn't have a name?

Looks like they don't trust us as much as we're willing to trust them.

Grunt continued. "Edward here has told us that the Atlantis gene was found written on the debris of a crashed UFO. Could you tell us a bit more about that, Edward? You mentioned that this document came up on the Pentagon server only last week, even though it's more than sixty years old. Could you tell us what you think about that?"

Edward was sitting on a stone, his dinner on a paper plate resting on his lap. Hearing his name, he stood up, dumping the steak and potatoes in the sand. He bent down to pick them up, burned his fingers on the steak, dropped it into the sand again, stood up again, bent down again, saw his meal was ruined, and finally gave up. Otto shook his head. That guy could hack into the Pentagon?

"Right, um," Edward started, looking mournfully down at his sandy dinner. "Well, you see..."

Edward's voice trailed off, and his entire body began to shake.

Otto's heart went out to him. He knew what was the matter. He'd seen it with some of the other residents at the group home. It was called Social Anxiety Disorder, something beyond shyness, a total fear of being in social situations.

People with Social Anxiety Disorder got panicky when they had to order a meal at a restaurant, and Edward was being asked to address a crowd of heavily armed strangers about secret documents he had stolen from the government.

Suddenly, Otto understood. Edward hid in a trailer in front of his computers because he felt safe there. Even with company in the room, his disorder didn't manifest because he was on safe ground. He was master of his little domain, the best hacker any of them knew. One of the best hackers in the world. A darknet superstar.

But at the moment, he was just an awkward guy trying to get the words out. And failing.

"Don't worry, man, just say it in your own time," Otto encouraged him. "Pretend you're in your trailer and you're making some wisecrack about how no one knows what's really going on except you."

Edward flashed him a nervous grin. It took him another few seconds to finally get started.

"The Pentagon has been..." Edward took a deep breath to steady himself and went on. "The Pentagon had been scanning and uploading old documents onto its server. It's a slow project. They have dozens of archivists working on it, but there are so many documents that have to be sifted through dating back decades, or even centuries, that it's taking ages."

Edward wiped his brow, took a breath, and continued. "So a document from 1947 being posted last week isn't unusual. What's unusual is its sensitive nature. Usually, highly classified documents like this are given first priority. I thought all the ones they planned on putting on the server were up there already."

Grunt looked about to ask a question, but seeing how much Edward was still trembling, he shut his mouth without saying a word. Edward didn't notice because his eyes were closed. He faced those in his audience without seeing them.

"This document was on the most secure server the Pentagon has. Some documents never make it onto a server because they don't want to risk even the smallest chance of their being hacked. Even on this server, there are five, maybe six hackers in the whole world who could get to it, and at least three of those are sellouts.

"But that's not the point. What's weird is that they put up something related to the Atlantis gene on the server at all. Anyone at that level has heard rumors that UFOs are real. Those who look at this document will either think it was some trick by an enemy power or will see evidence for what they believed was a real UFO crash all along. So it doesn't really change anything at the high levels of government, except for those who can see what Yuhle and I saw. I'm willing to bet whoever put that document up there was raising a signal to other people in the government who might be in the know. I'm thinking that, as usual with our government, there are a lot of little offices working in isolation from one another and wasting energy replicating each other's work. Organizations like the CIA, FBI, Homeland Security, and all the rest compete for funding, and there's a serious rivalry between them. They don't like to share information. Someone is trying to cut through all that and is calling for all the scattered groups to come together..."

Edward's final words were rushed. He still had his eyes closed, and his face was drenched with sweat that glowed in the reflected light of the campfire. He took a great gulp of air and said, "They're trying to get all their forces together, like us."

With that he sat, or practically fell, on the stone that he had been using for a chair.

"Thanks, Edward," Grunt said. "Now let's hear from Dr. Yamazaki. She's the leading expert on the Atlantis gene. In fact, she was the one who discovered it, and she's been discussing this all afternoon with Dr. Yuhle."

Dr. Yamazaki stood up, looking almost as nervous as Edward. She was still wearing the cheap dress and shoes she'd gotten from Goodwill and looked out of place among so many tough men and women who were well equipped for the desert.

She had good reason to look nervous. The Tohono O'odham were giving her stony looks, and there was none of the usual free joking as they had done with the other members of the Atlantis Allegiance. Grunt and Vivian looked at her with open distrust. Otto tried to keep his own features neutral. He still didn't know whether he could fully trust her or not, even after all they'd been through together.

Dr. Yamazaki brushed her long black hair out of her face and spoke.

"What Edward and Yuhle suspected is correct. The symbols in the report's picture match up with a portion of the sequence of the Atlantis gene. While I'm not saying I believe in UFOs, the fact that this is in a top secret government document is highly significant. When Yuhle and I were working on the Poseidon Project"—she turned to her old friend, who nodded and gave a supportive smile—"we sequenced the entire Atlantis gene. We still don't know what these particular genes do, because that takes years of study with a far bigger sample of people than we ever had. Perhaps whoever put up that sequence knows what it means, but that would mean there was a second Poseidon Project working without the knowledge of our own team. From what Edward says, it's possible. What do you think?"

She turned to where Edward had been sitting. He was gone.

Otto felt sorry for him. Once the meeting was over, he'd take some dinner to Edward's trailer.

After a pause, Dr. Yamazaki went on. "Well, anyway, it's impossible to know if they've figured out what the genes mean or not. Our team certainly didn't have the time to do it. When we were working for General Meade, I got the impression that he was always under pressure from his superior officers. He kept coming into the lab, asking for updates and wanting to know when certain goals would be met. And while he always got us any equipment we asked for, he seemed to fret about the expense."

One of the Tohono O'odham women called out, "Did he ever talk about UFOs or aliens?"

Dr. Yamazaki shook her head. "He never talked about anything that wasn't directly connected to our work. And I think I can anticipate your next question. The Atlanteans aren't aliens. They're human. Personally, I don't think there are aliens. I won't bore you with all the scientific details, but there are certain barriers in the laws of physics that keep a spaceship from going at the speed of light, and if you can't go faster than light speed, you'll never make it between the planets. The nearest star, Proxima Centauri, is four and a half light years away. So even if you were able to do the impossible, it would still take four and a half years to make it here from there, and Proxima Centauri doesn't even have any planets. The nearest exoplanet orbits around is Gliese 674 b, and that's fifteen light years away."

"But couldn't they have found a way we haven't figured out yet?" the woman asked.

Dr. Yamazaki shook her head. "Highly unlikely. I think UFO sightings are just a modernized form of religious experience, like people seeing angels or other spirits. UFOs are just a legend."

"Like Atlantis," Grunt said, his voice laden with sarcasm.

Dr. Yamazaki paused, apparently thinking, and then said, "In my research, I use the term 'Atlantis' as one of convenience. The genetic sequence is very old, dating to before the dawn of civilization ten thousand years ago. And my research seems to show that this sequence spread around the globe, like the original inhabitants of the legendary Atlantis. According to legend, their island sank, and the refugees brought their advanced civilization to all corners of the Earth. But I just use that term for convenience and to make a catchy title for my scientific papers. I don't believe there actually was an Atlantis."

"You're wrong," Jim Running Horse said.

Dr. Yamazaki cocked her head. "Am I?"

She had obviously regained her confidence since they were talking about something she knew so well.

"We've known of Atlantis from ancient times. It's one of the oldest stories of our people. And not just us but many other tribes as well. I've conferred with Hopi and Zuni elders and learned much from them that I didn't know. And they learned from me."

Dr. Yamazaki smiled and nodded. "Well, these stories are very important and need to be preserved, of course. What I mean to say is—"

Jim Running Horse held up a hand to stop her from going on.

"Don't give me that politically correct BS," he said. "You don't think any of our beliefs are real, and that's okay. If you want to treat people as equals, remember that equals disagree sometimes."

Dr. Yamazaki nodded and sat down. "You're right. I've spent too much time at universities where nobody is allowed to speak their minds. Everyone has to tiptoe around everyone else's feelings. Please go on."

"So you want me to entertain you with my quaint customs and charming fairy tales?" Jim Running Horse asked.

Otto couldn't tell if he was messing with her or not. He could pull such a perfectly straight face when he was joking that it was impossible to tell.

"I want you to tell me your oral history related to the Atlanteans," Dr. Yamazaki said. "There might be a clue as to where the Atlanteans came from."

"Aw, damn, I thought you were going to ask me to scalp the pyro over here." Jim Running Horse jabbed a thumb in Otto's direction. "That would have been much more fun!"

The Tohono O'odham all laughed, as did Grunt. Otto blushed.

Jim Running Horse moved near the fire, at the center of the circle.

"Okay, enough joking. I'm speaking of serious things now."

Everyone immediately fell silent. Otto glanced at Grunt and saw him facing his old friend with respect and deference. The expression looked strange on a face that was usually so cocky and sarcastic.

I'd love to learn more about the story between these two, Otto thought.

Jim Running Horse stood up straight and started to speak.

"We call them *hekhiu kekelbad*, which means 'old ancestors.' We say that instead of *kekelbad*, which means just 'ancestors' to distinguish them from our own forefathers. The *kekelbad* created our tribe, while the *hekhiu kekelbad* created many, many tribes. They weren't the first people, but they are among the first, and their blood runs in many people's veins. The legends say that they can be found in every part of the world.

"After the time of the First Man and First Woman, people spread all over the world and filled every corner of land. It's interesting that these old stories tell of things that the Tohono O'odham could never have seen. They tell how people moved far to the north to live in a place that was so cold the rain turned solid and people made houses out of this solid rain. They tell how people moved to the south and lived in a place where it was hot and rainy all the time, and the plants grew so thickly a person couldn't see as far as an arrow can shoot. The stories also tell how there was a big lake far to the east, and beyond this lake more land in which people lived in great houses made of stone. How could the Tohono O'odham have known of these things five hundred years ago? We have never traveled very far. These stories came to us from those who did.

"The old stories also tell of an island in the big lake, in what we now call the Atlantic Ocean. Very wise people lived on this island, some of the greatest descendants of the First Man and First Woman. Actually, the story doesn't say it was an island, it says it was the back of a giant turtle that lived in the lake, but you can't always take these old stories literally." Jim Running Horse smiled at Dr. Yamazaki. "These people became superhuman. They were stronger than a bear and faster than a deer. They were harder to kill than a mountain lion. Each of them also had a special ability. Some could heal the sick or had eyes like an eagle's. But each also had a weakness. Nothing too great but some minor flaw, as if the Creator wished to teach them to value all the gifts that He had given them."

Otto thought of Jaxon, with her ability to make plants grow and her frustration at not being able to read a simple sentence because of her dyslexia. It was eerie, sitting in the middle of the desert, listening to a Native American tell an old legend that described his girlfriend perfectly.

Jim Running Horse went on. "The story goes that the people of this island grew arrogant in their power and forgot that the Creator had tried to make them humble by giving each of them some flaw. Their society, once so pure and just, began to decay. Noble rulers were replaced with tyrannical despots, and their peaceful relations with their neighbors were replaced with conquest and bloodshed."

Otto nodded. Ever since he'd joined the Atlantis Allegiance, he'd been reading up on the old legends. Edward had a pile of books on Atlantis. A lot of the ridiculous claims sounded as if they had been made up by the authors in order to sell more copies, but there was a core of old stories from ancient Greece that sounded almost exactly like what he was hearing.

"The decay of the island people went on for some time, until the Creator at last lost his patience and decided to punish them. There was a terrible earthquake, and the island sank into the sea. Well, that's my interpretation. The story says the Creator painted some stones to look like lizard eggs, the turtle ate them, got a sore stomach, and swam down to the bottom of the lake to rest. Whatever happened, the island sank, and most of the people died. Some managed to get off and sail away on their boats. Then the Creator decided to punish them even more. He did not want them to establish a new kingdom somewhere else and repeat their evil, so he made all the Four Winds to blow at the same time. The boats were scattered to the four corners of the Earth. Ever since, small groups of Atlanteans could be found in every land, most of them unaware of their own heritage as they live as strangers in a foreign land they think is their own.

"Now you've probably heard much of this in your own stories. Most nations have stories like this that are only different in some details. But here's where it gets interesting. According to the Tohono O'odham history, and the histories I've heard from the Hopi and Zuni, the people of the island, who you call the Atlanteans, will come together again when the world is in danger. There will be signs in the sky and in the earth, signs in the water and signs of fire. The whole of humanity will face a grave danger, and the Atlanteans will have to come out of hiding and return to the noble ways they followed before the loss of their island. It will be the only hope for humanity."

Jim Running Horse sat down. There was silence around the circle for a time, and then everyone started talking quietly to their neighbors. Otto sat deep in thought. He wasn't sure how much of the old legend to believe. He'd seen and heard so many strange things since meeting Jaxon that he couldn't be sure of anything anymore.

Except for the fact that he desperately needed some sleep.

The meeting broke up. Some people went off to bed, while others hung out around the fire and finished their dinner. Otto's head hung low with fatigue. There had been too much excitement over the past couple of days and too little rest.

Suddenly, something caught his eye that made him perk up. One of the Tohono O'odham who had been sitting near him and smoking cigarettes got up and walked off, forgetting his lighter. Otto stared at it, sitting there on a log, just begging to be picked up. It never even occurred to him to tell the guy he had forgotten it.

Otto licked his lips and looked around. No one was paying any attention to him. No, he should leave it where it was.

Even as he was thinking that, he eased over and picked it up. He curled his fingers around it so no one could see what he was holding. The lighter felt new and full. Otto was an expert on lighters.

He slipped it in his pocket and felt a twinge of guilt. That was what his therapist called "slipping," when he'd fought off an addiction for a while and then went back to his old ways.

Otto sat back in his place and looked around. No, nobody had seen him. Weariness overcame him. He had to get some rest. With that lighter under his pillow, there would be some fine dreams tonight.

But he still had one thing left to do. He got a paper plate from the stack near the fire and loaded it up with a freshly cooked steak and a couple of potatoes. After grabbing a can of soda, he took the food over to Edward's trailer and knocked on the door.

No answer came. Otto put his ear to the door and could hear Edward furiously tapping away on the keyboard so loudly it almost sounded as if he were punching the keys. In the background, that strange shortwave radio station with the Slavic woman droned on.

"Eighty-nine...seven...twenty-three... five..."

Otto called out, "Edward, I have some dinner for you!"

The typing stopped for a moment, then resumed, faster and harder than before.

"I'll just leave it outside the door. Good night!"

Otto set the soda and food down in front of the door and stumbled away, looking for a place he could sleep.

Chapter 9

JUNE 20, 2016, ALBUQUERQUE,
NEW MEXICO

3:15 PM

General Meade couldn't believe his eyes. He was reading the recently digitized report that his assistant, Major Jefferson, had downloaded for him from the top secret Pentagon server, and it had been the most shocking thing he had ever seen.

The report was an addendum to the main report on the Roswell Incident, when the military had recovered a crashed UFO in New Mexico in 1947. The main report had been available in Pentagon circles for years and made absorbing reading. If the public saw it, they would have to accept the truth that aliens existed and were visiting the Earth.

Of course they would never see the report. It was classified top secret. Even he hadn't been given high enough clearance to read it or even know it existed until a couple of years ago. He would love to see the crashed flying saucer himself, but he'd have to be appointed to the Joint Chiefs of Staff or get elected president for that to happen.

So he had to content himself with reading about it in the old report.

And what a report. The main report, the one he had read years ago, detailed the vehicle and the alien bodies, plus some of the scientific research the team had performed at the time. No doubt there had been more recent tests with more advanced equipment since then, but Meade didn't get to know about that. It was frustrating to be one of the few high officers in the military to be serious about fending off the alien menace and not be allowed to know everything about it. It was like fighting blind.

But the new report added so much. It had been written a week after the first one, when a recovery team made a big sweep of the desert around the crash site. The alien craft had come in at a high velocity and low angle, and the front part of it had shattered on impact. Large amounts of debris were scattered for a good half mile around the site.

The recovery team had discovered some interesting bits of debris the first team had missed.

A photo of one piece had caught General Meade's eye. It was a thin strip of that unusual metal the aliens used for their craft, some alloy no one could identify. On it were printed some strange symbols. He immediately saw they weren't like the writing found on some other parts of the UFO, so he brought it over to his lead scientist in the Poseidon Project, Dr. Jones, to see what he thought. Of course he couldn't show Jones the full report, just that one photograph, but Jones was smart enough to know he was looking at something special.

Jones had stared at it for a moment, and his eyes bugged out. He had gone over to his computer, brought up the Atlantis genome, and showed General Meade how the symbols were actually codes for the building blocks of DNA and matched up with part of the Atlantis gene sequence.

The revelation almost made General Meade fall out of his chair. It took all of his self-restraint not to share what he knew with Dr. Jones. Instead, he staggered out of the lab and back to his office in a mental haze.

Part of the Atlantis gene was written on the wreckage of a UFO. What could it mean?

It couldn't be a fake, because nobody knew the structure of genes in 1947.

No one on Earth, anyway.

So were the Atlanteans alien? Dr. Jones, and Dr. Yamazaki before him, had insisted that the Atlanteans were human, that they shared virtually all the same genes as humans, only with a few additional ones. The reason he had tracked down Dr. Yamazaki in the first place was that she was using the Atlantean genes to trace the history of humanity. She had proven that there was a hidden branch of humanity that dated back unknown thousands of years and had spread throughout the world.

It would have been nice if she hadn't turned traitor. Then he wouldn't have had to dispose of her. She could have told him so much more than Dr. Jones.

So if the Atlanteans weren't alien, why was part of their genetic sequence depicted on an alien craft that had contained two Greys, those big-headed aliens with the giant eyes that the average member of the public thought were the only alien race visiting the Earth? Had the Atlanteans been some sort of alien genetic experiment?

General Meade sighed with frustration. So many questions and no answers. Dr. Jones wasn't the man to provide them either. He was half the scientist Dr. Yamazaki was.

Is, General Meade reminded himself. *She's back in the land of the living, and after what you did to her, she's twice as determined to take you down now. You have to get rid of her before she causes any more trouble.*

But he also needed to figure out what was going on with the Roswell report. He had been in the military too long to think that its appearance was simply a coincidence. Sure, new documents were being posted to the server all the time, but that one was too timely to be just random chance. It gave an important piece of the puzzle just when he was flailing around for answers.

General Meade logged onto his own computer, passed through the elaborate security protocol to get into the top secret server, and looked up the report. Each report on the server was digitally signed by the archivist who had uploaded it, any translators or other experts who had worked on it, and the commanding officer who had cleared it for release. The name of the commanding officer practically leaped off the screen at him—General Arnold Corbin of the United States Air Force.

Corbin had been his commanding officer when he had been stationed at Holloman Air Force Base near White Sands, New Mexico, back when Meade still thought extraterrestrials were fairy tales, and he and his military buddies laughed every time the experimental stealth bomber flew out of base and caused a wave of UFO sightings.

If he remembered correctly, General Corbin had been based in Roswell before that.

Intrigued, he looked up General Corbin's details of service, or at least those that were on the server. Meade's own resume omitted several things he'd been involved in. He suspected General Corbin's would be similarly incomplete.

It was complete enough. Before Roswell, General Corbin had been posted at the NATO headquarters in Brussels, Belgium, in 1989 and 1990, and before that, he had done a stint at the base in Rendlesham, England, through much of the 1980s. Both locations had stuck in General Meade's memory, even though he hadn't personally been to either of them. There had been a wave of sightings of huge triangular UFOs all over Belgium that was unprecedented in the number of witnesses and confirmed Air Force radar contacts. As for Rendlesham, that was the site of one of the most important UFO sightings in England, when United States Air Force personnel investigated some strange lights in the woods near the base and saw a glowing, multicolored object passing between the trees. Both Belgium and Rendlesham counted as two of the most convincing UFO cases in recent decades.

And General Corbin had been there for both of them.

General Meade leaned back in his chair and let out a long, slow breath.

This is a signal, he thought. *He wants me to get in touch.*

In his early days as a UFO believer, General Meade had made a bit of a fool of himself. He had pestered his colleagues about any clues they might have and raved to anyone who would listen about how aliens were real. Several sarcastic remarks and a quiet word from one of his superior officers made him realize that some beliefs shouldn't be broadcast too loudly. He learned to keep them to himself, searching out those who might have information or a sympathetic ear and approaching them only if he was sure it wouldn't hurt his career. As in any other line of work, a person's chances at promotion in the military relied just as much on their image as their ability.

So had General Corbin heard about his interest in UFOs, somehow heard about the Poseidon Project, and decided it was time to put the document on the top secret server where he knew General Meade was sure to see it?

"Only one way to find out," General Meade said to himself, reaching for the phone.

When he got through, he found General Corbin friendly, eager to talk, and completely unsurprised to receive his call. That only confirmed Meade's suspicions that the report's release was a signal to anyone who might be interested in the UFO menace. Meade was careful not to speak too much on the phone, however. He'd been judged for his interests too many times before.

When General Corbin suggested he come down and visit him at his current posting in Virginia, General Meade ground his teeth. Another long flight that the bureaucrats in Washington would want justified. Well, hang them. It was important, and Corbin obviously didn't want to talk over the phone any more than he did.

Two days later, General Meade was passing through the gates of Langley Air Force Base in Virginia. Barracks stood in long rows off to one side, and a large warehouse on the other side lay open as mechanics worked on several tanks. The road led through the base, past columns of jogging soldiers and a row of artillery being towed away by Hummers, probably to the gunnery range that General Meade knew was attached to the base.

Meade parked his government rental car in front of the administration building and checked in at the front desk. The sergeant on duty gave him a sloppy salute that Meade decided to ignore. The sergeant was Air Force, Meade was Army. The different branches of service had deep-seated rivalries, something Meade thought was stupid and dangerous.

Conflict between different agencies in both the civilian government and the armed forces had led to numerous security lapses over the years, including 9/11, and some fumbled battles in overseas wars, not to mention countless millions of wasted dollars. General Corbin had been the man to teach him that all branches of service needed to work together for the good of the country.

Back when Meade was a rising young officer stationed at White Sands, he got a lot of ribbing for being one of the few Army officers on an Air Force base, but none of that ribbing ever came from Corbin. He had always welcomed soldiers from other branches of the military, saying they all needed to work together.

That welcoming attitude did not extend to members of the civilian government. Like many high-ranking officers, Meade included, Corbin didn't trust the spooks from the CIA or the rednecks from ATF. People shouldn't have military powers unless they had military training.

After going through security, General Meade was led to General Corbin's office and was ushered inside.

Corbin was much as he remembered him—a rugged, aging Vietnam veteran who had earned a Purple Heart and a Silver Star in the line of duty. He stood rigidly erect and gave Meade a firm handshake.

"Good to see you again, Hector," Corbin said, using Meade's first name with a familiarity typical of him. "Glad you could make it. Please sit down. How can I help you?"

Meade paused. How to start? He remembered Corbin was a direct person, so he might as well be direct.

"As I mentioned on the phone, I saw your work in getting some old documents scanned and uploaded onto the Armed Forces Top Secret Server. I'm sure you're aware of my interest in this subject."

General Corbin smiled. "'Martian Meade,' I think that's what they used to call you, isn't it?"

General Meade grimaced. He hadn't heard that nickname in years. Perhaps people still called him that behind his back and he didn't know. It was not something a private would say to a general's face, after all.

Corbin seemed to read his thoughts. "I'm sure people say the same sort of things when I'm not around too, but they're idiots. You know as well as I do that the alien threat is real."

General Meade leaned forward. Suddenly they were getting to the heart of the matter. "I've read everything I can in the secret reports. The sightings are getting more frequent, and closer. Do you think they're preparing for an invasion?"

Corbin nodded. "It certainly seems so. I don't think they're ready to strike just yet, but they are definitely ramping up their activity. We need to be prepared."

The Air Force general paused, as if waiting for Meade to speak.

You want me to say it first, don't you? Meade thought. *It looks like I'm the one who has to take the risk of exposing myself. Remind me never to play poker with you.*

Meade took a deep breath and said, "We need a breed of super soldiers, people with superior genetics. It's the only way to fight back."

Corbin looked at him with interest but continued to keep silent.

Meade steeled himself and went on. "There is such a group of people. Some scientists think they are descended from the people of Atlantis." General Corbin shifted in his seat, and Meade hurried to add, "But I'm not sure of that. They certainly are genetically superior, though. That's not in doubt."

General Meade felt a deep sense of embarrassment. Hearing his old nick-name—"Martian Meade"—had brought back some bad memories. He hated being laughed at. On the surface, some of his beliefs sounded ridiculous, as though he was some wild-eyed civilian spending too much time on the Internet rather than behaving as a high-ranking general. The fact that the alien threat was real and hardly anyone believed it made the laughter doubly hurtful. And there he was talking about the lost continent of Atlantis.

General Corbin fiddled with a pen on his desk and said in a low voice, "The Air Force has been studying the Atlantean theory."

Meade perked up. That was what he had suspected all along.

"You have a research project?" he asked.

General Corbin nodded. "We've had one for a few years now. I can't give you very many details, just like you can't give me many details about the project you're involved in. You know how different branches of service are always keeping secrets from one another. It's like if you gave my three kids four slices of pizza. Who gets the extra one? Everyone is always fighting over funding instead of fighting our enemies. It's a national disgrace."

"I'm willing to cooperate as much as I can as long as I don't have to release any classified information you aren't privy to," Meade stated.

General Corbin shook his head. "I wouldn't ask you to. Let's go through what I can tell you. First off, you're right about the alien reconnaissance. The Air Force is better placed to study that than the Army, and we've gathered some disturbing data. The UFOs are beginning to focus on the nation's main sources of energy—not just nuclear plants like they did when we first started building them back in the fifties but also hydroelectric dams, coal plants, even wind and solar farms. From what we can gather from our allies, it's happening in other countries too."

"Our energy grid? That would be a strategic target to hit if they were planning an invasion, but perhaps they want it for other purposes."

General Corbin nodded. "That's what the researchers here at the Air Force are thinking. Maybe they want to take the energy from our planet for some reason.

Now about the Atlanteans. From rumors I hear, you've been studying the Atlantis gene. That's why I put up that Roswell report, because I wanted to see if you would spot the significance. You didn't disappoint me. It seems your project is fairly advanced. Our project has been more modest but has been going on for some years. We've been studying the DNA of Atlantean servicemen and servicewomen."

General Meade's brow furrowed. "Is that so? We've been looking through the American population and found that Atlanteans almost never join the armed forces. They tend to lie low. Enlisting would make them stand out."

"Ah, but you forget the draft. We've been gathering DNA samples from patients in Veterans Administration hospitals. We assembled a list of all mixed-race draftees from World War Two, the Korean War, and Vietnam and got DNA samples from them, telling them it was part of whatever treatment they had come into the hospital for. Many turned out to simply be mixed race, but we've assembled a database of more than six hundred Atlanteans."

General Meade's eyes went wide. "Six *hundred*? That's remarkable! Our team had no idea they were that common."

"Well, I wouldn't say *common*. Six hundred out of a sample size of more than a million, but it's a skewed sample. First off, it doesn't include women since women have never been eligible for the draft. Plus the sample only covers draftees from three wars who have come into the VA hospital. The actual number of Atlanteans in America must be in the thousands, maybe even the tens of thousands."

General Meade sat back in awe. That changed everything. He could assemble more than a strike team, he could assemble a real army.

"How could so many have gone unde-tected? My God, sir, why haven't they taken over?" General Meade thought for a moment, then snapped his fingers. "Our sampling has been wrong! We've been looking for mixed-race individuals who show remarkable physical ability. What if not all Atlanteans have these traits?"

General Corbin nodded. "Now you're on the right track. You almost have it. In fact, all Atlanteans do have supernatural physical powers, but they don't always manifest themselves. In fact, they rarely do. Most Atlanteans go their whole lives without realizing they're special."

General Meade rubbed his jaw. "I wonder if there's a way to bring out those abilities."

"There is."

"How?"

General Corbin sighed. "I'm afraid that's classified."

"How are we going to work together if we can't freely communicate?"

General Corbin frowned. "I'm not sure. The bureaucrats in Washington don't want us to cooperate. They've always needed the military, but they fear us too. So they play these games with funding. It's the old 'divide and conquer' tactic."

"This is no time for petty civilian politics!" General Meade thundered. "We need to act."

General Corbin's eyes narrowed. "We took an oath to defend this nation against all enemies, foreign and domestic. I intend to keep that oath."

"So do I," General Meade replied, and then paused. There had been something in Corbin's tone, a hardness, a determination, that told him he wasn't going to let anyone stop him. And had he placed a slight emphasis on the word "domestic"?

General Meade cocked his head and studied his senior officer. Just what was the man getting at? He thought he knew, but he didn't dare put it into words.

He felt it, though. The civilian government had been holding the military back for far too long. It was their lack of will that had made them lose Vietnam and Lebanon and Somalia. Those fights had been winnable. A military leader would have won them. But time and again, the politicians and bureaucrats in Washington had tripped up the military.

As humiliating as those defeats had been, they were nothing compared to what would happen if America lost its war with the aliens. The country, all of humanity, would lose everything. Humans might even become extinct.

What was that line an officer fighting in Vietnam had said?

"We had to destroy this village in order to save it."

General Meade saw clearly then. Begging for funding and sneaking around behind the government's back wouldn't get him the resources he needed, not in the time frame they were looking at. He had to go further, and General Corbin was hinting he was willing to go further too.

Both of them wanted to save America, and if that meant destroying its democratic institutions for a time, then so be it. Better to have a living military dictatorship than a dead country.

General Meade extended a hand across Corbin's desk.

"Sir, I think we're of the same mind. Let's start talking frankly. We have a war to win."

Chapter 10

JUNE 27, 2016, LOS ANGELES,
CALIFORNIA

11:00 AM

Jaxon couldn't believe her luck. She had told her foster parents that she wanted to take the bus to meet some of her friends in downtown Hollywood, and they had actually let her go. Stephen and Isadore seemed eager for her to make friends at her new school and didn't ask too many questions. That was fine by Jaxon. She didn't want to answer questions about which friends she was going to meet or what they were going to do. That would have been hard to answer.

Hard to answer because Jaxon had no friends, and she wasn't going to be meeting anyone.

She really was going to downtown Hollywood, though. Long ago, Jaxon had learned that telling too many lies soon got confusing, and it was best, if she were going to garnish the truth a little, to leave in enough truth that she could keep track of her own story.

Jaxon tried not to think how pathetic it was to lie about having friends. She was used to not having any, and while it was lonely, she didn't want to talk about it. Isadore, with that fake enthusiasm she always showed when she was trying to act like a supportive mother, would only encourage her to try harder.

If her foster parents wanted her to have friends, they should have sent her to a different school. The kids at hers were as fake as their nose jobs. Maybe she was naive, but she had never seen a teenager with plastic surgery before, and at her new school, it was hard to find one who hadn't had some, even among the boys.

Jaxon sat on the bus as it rolled through the city, gazing out at the long stretches of residential neighborhoods and strip malls and gas stations, all looking alike. She shook her head. The city was as fake as the kids at her school. All glitz and glamour with no heart, like that neighbor of hers with the big, rich house, the man who liked to beat up prostitutes. Briefly, Jaxon felt worried that he would notice she lived on the same block. He might be looking for payback.

After a moment, Jaxon stopped worrying. The guy was a loser, and if she could beat him up once, she could beat him up a second time. It wasn't as though he was going to call the police. What would he tell them?

They were passing an office building with a thin strip of grass between the sidewalk and parking lot, a pathetic attempt at making it look as though the place had a front yard. Jaxon spotted a man in overalls who had a big metal container attached to a sprayer that was shooting out a fine mist of green paint onto the grass.

Curious, Jaxon turned in her seat to watch as they passed. She heard a laugh behind her.

A young black man sitting nearby said, "You must be new to LA, sister."

"Um, yeah. What was he doing?"

"Painting the grass green. It's gone all brown. Because of the drought, watering lawns has been banned."

Jaxon shook her head and laughed. "So they're painting the grass?"

"Welcome to LA, sister! It's like we're all in the movies."

Jaxon sat back in her seat and smiled. Yeah, the whole city was fake. Maybe it was the place for her, because didn't she put up a false front too? She had been doing it all her life, at least since she found out about her powers. She had to when she knew she didn't belong. That guy had called her "sister," seeing her black skin and nothing else. Oh, maybe he noticed she was part white and Asian too, but he chose to see her as black.

Jaxon didn't see herself as black. She didn't see herself as any race, not even mixed race. It was weird, but for some reason, she never thought of herself as mixed, although one look in the mirror told her she was. It was obvious, and yet it didn't feel right. She could fake it and call that guy "brother," but she didn't feel any more a part of his race than she did of anyone else's.

Which made her doubly annoyed when people at school made racist comments. Not only was it lame to make those jokes, but also it was twice as lame to think they applied to her.

The bus was driving along Hollywood Boulevard. The Chinese Theatre appeared off to their left, the famous cinema palace with its amazing dragon facade that looked as if it had been brought over from medieval China. Jaxon decided to get off there.

"Going to see the sights?" the guy behind her asked.

"Meeting someone," she said with a smile. The guy looked disappointed. He had his phone in his hand. Then he put it back in his pocket. Jaxon guessed he had been about to ask for her number. Well, lying about having friends turned out to be useful on more than just her foster parents. She favored him with a goodbye smile and got off the bus.

The chance encounter on the bus put her in a good mood as she strolled down Hollywood Boulevard. Not many guys tried to pick her up, because she wasn't exactly pretty, and some people had problems with her being mixed race. Otto always said he liked her blend of features.

Otto. What was he doing? Working on some chain gang? Exercising in the prison yard? She hoped he was okay. She'd heard all sorts of horror stories about prison. A gentle heart like Otto didn't deserve to behind bars with a bunch of carjackers and killers.

Jaxon sighed. There didn't seem to be anything she could do. She was tempted to write him but was afraid her foster parents would object. No one had told her what prison he'd been assigned to, so she didn't even know where to write anyway.

She set her shoulders and tried to put those dark thoughts out of her mind. It was a bright, sunny day, not too hot, and she had managed to grab a few hours of freedom for herself. Good times were rare in her life, and she shouldn't waste them. Today she was going to enjoy herself.

She loitered around the front of the Chinese Theatre, looking at all the hand-prints placed in the concrete by movie stars. It was an old Hollywood tradition for stars and directors to get a wet slab of concrete and put their handprints and footprints in it. Some were made all the way back in the 1920s. A lot of the older names she didn't recognize, although she'd heard of Clark Gable and of course Marilyn Monroe. She was surprised to see Jack Nicholson's prints dated to 1974. How old was that guy? She also saw prints of Arnold Schwarzenegger—who'd written above his handprints, "I'll be back"—Johnny Depp, Michael Jackson, and Sandra Bullock.

Next she saw the Walk of Stars and then the Wax Museum. She found that a bit creepy. Not the Chamber of Horrors, which was lame, but just the idea of a wax museum. All of those wax dummies were made to look like famous people. She took a couple of selfies and then found herself deleting them. They were too weird. Fake people. Didn't she have enough of those in her life?

She sent one photo to her foster parents so they would know she hadn't lied about where she was going.

Jaxon liked the *Ripley's Believe It Or Not! Odditorium* better. The Darth Vader made of scrap metal was cool, and the woman who could pop her eyes out of her head made Jaxon feel much more normal. The guy with the twenty-eight-foot fingernails made Jaxon feel the woman with the pop-out eyes was normal too.

Afterward she got lunch at Musso & Frank Grill, Hollywood's oldest surviving restaurant. The day was really turning out great. She couldn't remember the last time she had been able to spend so much time alone. The only people who talked to her were a couple of guys who tried to hit on her like that guy in the bus.

She couldn't figure out why they bothered. They were cool about it and took the hint that she wanted to be alone, but she'd never had so much attention before. Usually guys walked right past her.

Maybe it was her confidence. That had been growing. Could it be that they sensed that and it made her more attractive?

After lunch, she strolled down a side road, wondering what was just off the famous boulevard. She walked for a long time without really paying much attention to where she was going, simply daydreaming about movie stars and enjoying the peaceful solitude.

Suddenly she became aware that she no longer knew where she was.

Damn, how had she managed that? That cheap old phone of hers didn't even have GPS, and she didn't have a WiFi signal to check any map. The street she was on was certainly no tourist attraction. Instead of famous movie theatres and wax museums, it had liquor stores and pawnshops. Everyone there looked a bit run-down, like the buildings. One guy going the other way stared at her chest as he passed.

She needed to get to a better neighborhood.

A cry from an alley to her right made her turn. At the far end of the alley, past heaps of trash and some stains Jaxon didn't want to identify, she saw a fight going on. Three teenagers were cheering and laughing as they beat on someone staggering between them.

Jaxon hesitated. Should she help? But the fight wasn't like the one between her neighbors and the prostitute. That had been clear-cut. But at that moment, she didn't know which side was right.

Except that it was three against one. She'd been bullied like that before. But what if the guy was a thief who had robbed them?

She stood, uncertain, at the opening to the alley. None of them noticed her. The guy in the middle was getting smacked around pretty badly by the teenagers, although every once in a while, he got a hit in and one of them would stumble backward.

Then the people shifted, and she got a good look at who the teenagers were fighting.

He was an older man with an unkempt beard turning gray. He wore a dirty overcoat and shoes that were so worn-out that his bare toes stuck through the front. The guy was homeless.

Jaxon took a couple of steps into the alley and opened her mouth to shout at them to stop.

Just then, a figure in a hooded sweatshirt ran around the far end of the alley. She hadn't noticed before that it took a left turn around the building she stood next to. At first, she thought it had been a dead end.

The figure leaped into the fray, knocking down one of the teenagers with a martial arts kick. Then he swung around and landed a punch right on the nose of the second teen, knocking him back so that he cracked his head on the brick wall of the alley and slumped down, unconscious. The third teen took a swing at the newcomer and cracked him in the jaw. The hood fell away, and Jaxon gasped. It was Brett, a guy from her class!

Brett shook off the blow, managed to block another punch, and gave the teen a straight kick to the groin that doubled him up and left him groaning on the pavement.

Brett turned and started talking to someone tucked in a doorway and almost hidden from her view. In all the excitement, Jaxon hadn't noticed that person. Brett extended his open hand. It didn't look as though he was about to attack. It looked as though he was demanding something.

"Brett!" Jaxon called out.

At the sound of his name, Brett turned, his eyes widening and his jaw dropping as he recognized her.

The figure in the doorway popped out behind him and ran down the alley.

"Damn!" Brett shouted, running after the figure.

Jaxon headed down the alley too. The homeless man was leaning against the alley wall, wiping his bleeding nose. One of the teens who had attacked him was just getting up. Jaxon knocked him back down again as she passed.

Brett grabbed the figure who was running away and spun around. The figure staggered for a second. Jaxon saw it was a girl about her age holding a cell phone.

"She was filming the whole thing!" Brett shouted.

The girl swore at them and whined, "We were only having some fun!"

Brett managed to grab the phone from her hand. "Don't move," he ordered and took a look at her phone. Then it was his turn to swear. He held up the phone so Jaxon could see.

The video app was on, and it was live streaming to a website called beatingthebums.com. Suddenly Jaxon felt ill.

"What the hell is this?" she demanded.

"Trouble," Brett said. He smashed the phone against the wall several times until it was dead. "She got my face, and probably yours too, and thanks to you, she got my name."

The sound of running feet made them turn. The girl was disappearing around the corner.

"Let her go," Brett said. "I don't hit girls, not even ones like her."

"What's going on?" Jaxon asked.

The homeless man staggered up to them. His nose was still bleeding, and one eye was beginning to swell shut.

"Thank you so much, sir," the man said, sending a cloud of alcohol fumes over Brett and Jaxon. "Those little bastards have been attacking a lot of guys lately."

"And they put it up on the Internet?" Jaxon asked, appalled.

"Yup. Think it's funny," the homeless man said. "Well, their viewers got an eyeful today, didn't they? Har har!"

"Too much of an eyeful," Brett grumbled.

"But what are you doing here?" Jaxon asked.

Brett shrugged. "Just hanging out."

"In a back alley in a bad part of town?"

"Well, what are you doing here?"

"I got lost."

A thud and a groan made them turn. The homeless man had given one of his attackers a kick and was walking out into the street.

"Thanks again, man. You're a real hero!" he called back to Brett before rounding the corner and disappearing from view.

Something clicked in Jaxon's mind. She spun to face Brett. "Wait, you're that guy in the papers!"

Brett grinned and stretched out his arms. "The same! You never suspected you were dating a superhero, did you?"

"Um, we're not dating."

"Of course we are. But before I take you out on our next date, let's get out of this alley. I don't feel like fighting these guys again once they wake up. Besides, this place smells like the school bathroom."

They headed out onto the street as the teenagers slowly picked themselves up. Brett led her back to a nicer part of town.

"So why are you doing this?" Jaxon asked.

Brett shrugged. "I'm bored, and there's too much injustice in the world. Helpless people are always getting stepped on, and I felt it was time to do something about it. But mostly I'm bored."

"You became an imitation Superman because you're bored."

Brett turned to her and tried to put an arm around her waist. Jaxon stepped back, and he ended up hooking empty air.

"Glad you think I'm Superman, baby. Are you Lois Lane?"

"Comic books are stupid."

Brett inclined his head in the direction from which they had come.

"Nothing stupid about knocking down trash like that. You know how I knew about these guys? Courtney sent a video from beatingthebums.com to a bunch of us. She thinks it's hilarious."

"Why am I not surprised."

They continued walking. Brett tried to put an arm around her, and she ducked away again. For a minute, they walked in silence, Jaxon's mind racing. There she was walking next to the guy who had inspired her own night walks, and it turned out to be a spoiled kid from school.

How could someone on the golf team be a superhero?

They'd gone on a date a while back. Basically, he had pestered her until she said yes. It hadn't been so bad. Brett was superficial and kind of dumb, but at least he treated her like a human being. That was more than she could say about the other kids at school.

And suddenly, Brett had become interesting.

"So tell me more about this vigilante thing," she said.

"It doesn't freak you out, does it?" Brett said, looking concerned.

Jaxon shook her head slowly. "No, but I'm surprised you'd do it."

Brett bit his lip. "Yeah, I figured you'd say something like that. It would probably surprise everyone I know. I've always been a bit of a screwup. My older sister is smarter than I am, got a full ride to Princeton. And my dad is a big overachiever. Mom is popular in society, running all sorts of charities and stuff, and what do I have? A decent golf game and a winning smile."

"You don't have a winning smile."

"Well, I'm pretty good at golf, though," Brett said and laughed.

Brett always laughed at everything. It was one of his more annoying traits. That time, though, his laughter sounded fake.

"I got the idea to do vigilante stuff from this cheesy old TV show my dad made me watch that he loved as a kid. It's called *The Greatest American Hero*. It's about some loser who dresses up as a superhero and fights crime. It's all very eighties. I mean, the guy's got a *perm*! I can't believe men really did that back then. Anyway, it got me to thinking. The guy is a total nobody in his regular life, but his superhero persona becomes famous and saves a lot of people. And I figured, why not do this for real?"

"You became a vigilante because of an old TV show?"

"No, I became a vigilante because I wanted to be somebody."

"I thought you said you did it because you were bored."

Brett stopped and looked her in the eye. "Yeah, bored with myself. Bored with living in a house so big that I can walk from one end to another without bumping into any of my family. Bored with the fact that I don't want to bump into them. Bored with school. Bored with people like Courtney. Bored with people calling me a spoiled rich brat when they're the happy ones. Bored with pretty much everything."

Jaxon was taken aback. She'd never heard him speak seriously about anything before. Brett grinned again. That time, it didn't look so forced.

"So I got the idea to come out and fight crime. I've been taking Wing Chung Kung Fu since I was a kid. As you can see, I'm even better at that than golf. It gives me a thrill to walk through these crappy neighborhoods. There's always someone to protect. It makes me feel useful. Did you read those articles about me in the paper?"

"Yeah."

"Those are only two of my latest jobs. I've done plenty more. Newspapers are always slow to pick up on stuff."

They'd gotten back on Hollywood Boulevard and slowly walked past the tourist spots Jaxon had admired that morning. Brett waved a hand at all the glittering signs and ornate buildings.

"This is the only LA most people want to see, and I'm not just talking about the tourists but privileged people like us too. Most people live in crappy parts of town and are always afraid. They deserve better. So maybe I'm doing a bit of good."

Jaxon shook her head. It was so hard to believe.

"What?" Brett asked, noticing her gesture.

"Nothing."

"What?"

Jaxon laughed. "I guess I'm just weirded out that I can't look down on you anymore."

"You looked down on me?" Brett seemed hurt.

"You got to admit that you don't make a very good impression."

"I don't? Well, now that you've met the real me…"

Brett hooked his arm around Jaxon's waist.

"Brett, since you're a vigilante, could you help me?"

Brett's face turned serious. "What, are you in trouble?"

"Yeah, there's this creepy guy at school…"

"Who?" Brett demanded.

"…he's always bothering me, trying to get close and always asking me out…"

"Who is the bastard? I'll take care of him!"

"…he's not a bad guy. He just won't take no for an answer. He's always trying to grab me."

"What a creep. I'll pulverize him for you."

"He's a bit boring too. Oh, he's got a more interesting side to him, but then he'll come off all fake and start talking about golf."

Brett's hand fell from her waist. He had a glum face like a kid who had just been denied an ice cream cone.

"Sounds like you can take care of yourself," he grumbled.

Jaxon laughed bitterly. "Oh, if only I could!"

Chapter 11

JUNE 28, 2016, TUCSON, ARIZONA

6:45 PM

Otto was beginning to wonder if everyone in the Atlantis Allegiance was going to spend the rest of their lives hiding out in the desert. They'd spent the first three days in the remote hideout near Yuma, in a desolate stretch of sand and rock far from any settlement or even a gas station.

Most of that time, he didn't have anything to do. Edward had been buried in his online research, trying to find more evidence of Atlanteans or the Atlantis gene in old UFO reports. Grunt and Vivian played soldier with the Tohono O'odham in the hills nearby, making sure no one came close to their settlement, and Drs. Yuhle and Yamazaki mostly conferred between themselves, occasionally braving the funky smell in Edward's trailer to look at documents the hacker had found.

From what they said, they weren't finding much of interest. Still, Otto envied them. At least they had something to do. Edward wouldn't let him get on the Internet for fear he'd get tracked, and after reading a couple of dog-eared old paperbacks one of the Native Americans had in his pickup truck, Otto was excruciatingly bored.

A little excitement came on the fourth day when they moved the entire camp to another location, that time in the Sonora Desert in South Central Arizona. They hid in a little side canyon of the Santa Rita Mountains, surrounded by towering saguaros, those strange cacti that looked like green, prickly people holding their arms in the air. By day there were buzzards and rattlesnakes, by night owls and scorpions. On the first night, one of the Tohono O'odham had loaned him a handheld black light.

"What's this for?" Otto had asked.

"Switch it on, and let's go for a walk," the man had replied. He led Otto to a cluster of rocks. "Shine the light over there."

Otto did as he was told, panning the beam across the jagged rocks. The lamp lit on a weird, glowing neon-blue oval. Otto peered closer and saw that it was a scorpion.

"Wow," Otto said. "Neat trick."

"Keep looking," the man told him.

Otto searched the rocks and found three more scorpions clustering on them.

"Keep that with you," the Tohono O'odham advised. "Scorpions like to come out at night when it's cooler. The smaller, clear ones are the most venomous. They're called bark scorpions and are the only ones that come in groups. My neighbor got stung once, said it hurt more than when he broke his leg as a kid. He was seeing double until they got him to the hospital and pumped him full of antivenom. If you're going to wander around at night, shine that ahead of you. Also, check your trailer and sleeping bag before you turn in."

Otto figured that was a good idea. The first night was a bit tense, checking for the little poisonous critters everywhere. By the next day, however, he'd fallen into the same dull routine, and he began to lose hope that they'd ever do anything interesting again, so when Vivian told him they were meeting someone in Tucson for dinner, someone who might have some clues to what was going on, Otto leaped at the chance to go. People! Shops! A meal at a restaurant! It sounded way better than another cookout and a couple of hours looking at the stars until he was tired enough to go to sleep.

Besides Vivian, most of the core team were also going—Drs. Yamazaki and Yuhle, and Grunt. Otto was surprised to see they were taking Dr. Yamazaki along. The others must have decided she could be trusted enough for the meeting. Another decision they had taken without him. Sometimes he wondered why he was even there.

Edward said he had things to do and stayed in his trailer, set up at the base of a forty-foot cactus. From a distance, the cactus rising up behind the hacker's trailer looked like a giant green radio antenna.

Otto sat in the back of the car with the two scientists. Dr. Yamazaki looked happy to be going into town.

"I had a postdoc at the university here," she said.

"A postdoc?" Otto asked.

"That's a research position you get right after graduating."

"That's cool."

Dr. Yuhle laughed. "Cool if you like short-term, underpaid grunt work. But at least it gets you started."

As the car neared the city's nightglow to the west, Dr. Yamazaki described the land they were going through.

The thin range of small, jagged mountains that their two-lane road snaked through to the east of town was called the Rincons. It didn't take long to get through them, and the land opened up into a vast bowl of a valley.

They hit it at exactly the right time of day. The sun had just winked out behind the low range of the Tucson Mountains that made up the valley's western edge. To the north stood an imposing wall of mountains Dr. Yamazaki told him were called the Catalinas. The sunset had turned the mountains a deep gold that within a few minutes turned into a brilliant crimson. The tops of many of the peaks were darkened by trees. Pointing off to the left toward the south, she showed him the distant Santa Rita Mountains, which looked as though they might be the biggest of them all.

Before them stretched the lights of Tucson, taking up almost the entire valley. Dr. Yamazaki wrinkled her nose.

"When I worked here in the nineties, the city was only a little more than half this size. Every year, developers ripped up more desert to add new housing that looked like it had come out of a cookie cutter. I used to love hiking around Tucson. You could get to a good trailhead in twenty minutes from any part of the city, even from downtown. But now? I wonder how many canyons like the one we're camping in have been wiped out."

Otto had never been to Tucson before, so when they drove into the city, he took a close look around him, wondering if that would be a good place to hide out. He smiled when he realized he was looking at everything in terms of survival. His old life was only a few weeks in the past, and yet he felt as if it had been lived by another person.

The town itself looked a bit like Los Angeles, with long strip malls, low apartment buildings clustered around swimming pools, and lots of single-story houses. The town became more interesting when they got to the old center, with a real trolley and some old adobe houses left over from another era. They ended up at a Mexican restaurant where the walls were decorated with colorful striped blankets and old photos of Mexican ranchers and revolutionaries. Half the diners were speaking Spanish.

"I haven't been here in ages," Dr. Yamazaki said as a waitress brought bowls of nachos and salsa. "This is Sonoran food. I hope you like cheese and refried beans."

"This salsa is awesome," Otto said, digging into it with some nachos.

"And there's free refills on that," she said with a smile, scooping up some hot sauce with her own corn chip. "But save some room for the main course. You'll love it."

They sat for a few minutes, waiting, with Otto and Dr. Yamazaki finishing off the bowl of nachos and ordering another, while Grunt and Vivian studied the crowd and Dr. Yuhle enjoyed a margarita. Suddenly Dr. Yamazaki squealed with delight and leaped up to embrace an old man who had entered the restaurant. He had snow-white hair in a thin fringe around his head, and was pale and thin with advanced old age, but he still walked with a steady energy and gave Dr. Yamazaki a wide grin when she embraced him.

"I knew you'd pick this place," the old man said and laughed.

Dr. Yamazaki turned to address the team. "Everyone, I'd like you to meet Dr. Charles Smith. He was my boss during my postdoc here."

"Watching how your career developed, it made me proud to be there at the beginning." He sat down next to Dr. Yamazaki.

"Dr. Smith was one of the first experts in generational genetics, tracing the ancestry of human populations. He can help us learn more about—"

Otto raised a hand to silence her. Dr. Yamazaki stared at him for a second, then nodded and stopped talking. Vivian and Grunt gave him approving looks.

Great, Otto thought. *I'm getting as paranoid as them. Probably a good idea, though.*

Dinner came, and they tucked into massive burritos and enchiladas slathered in melted cheese. Otto had to admit that while being in the Atlantis Allegiance had made him a wanted fugitive and had gotten him shot at more than once, at least he got to eat well.

Dr. Yamazaki ate very well. She downed her own burrito, part of Otto's, more chips and salsa, and ordered some side dishes too. Otto wondered where she put it all. She ate more than Grunt, while keeping up a constant conversation with her old professor. Most of it was technical stuff that went over his head, but he could tell the older scientist was proud of his former student.

Once they finished their meal, they agreed to go back to Dr. Smith's house, tucked away in the Tucson Mountains to the west of town. Dr. Smith gave them detailed directions, so they wouldn't have to turn on their GPS, and concluded by saying, "And if Otto here would be so kind as to drive my car for me, that would be a big help. My night vision isn't what it used to be."

"I'd be happy to, Dr. Smith."

Grunt whispered something in Dr. Yamazaki's ear. She got an annoyed look and told the professor, "I need to talk to them about something. I'll ride in our car."

Dr. Smith nodded and smiled. "Okay, Akiko. See you at the house."

Smith's car was a classic old Cadillac from the fifties that looked as though it was worth a fair chunk of change. It had been lovingly preserved and painted a gleaming gold color. Otto drove with care. He decided it would be a bad idea to tell Dr. Smith about some of the recent drives he'd been on. He'd hate to see government agents put bullets through that beauty. Maybe the St. Christopher medal hanging from the rearview mirror would save the paint job.

"Nice car, professor. I bet that paint job looks great at sunset."

"It does at that. I always wanted a car like this when I was your age but never had the money. By the time I could afford one, I was well into middle age and would have looked like I was trying to recapture my youth. Now I'm ninety-one and don't care. That's one of the benefits of growing old that no one tells you about. After a certain point, you stop caring what other people think."

"That would be nice," Otto said. He'd been dealing with other people's opinions all his life.

"You seem rather the odd man out, if you don't mind my saying so. How do you fit into this picture?"

Otto shook his head and smiled. "That's complicated."

"Complicated in the sense that many factors have intervened in order to bring about a chain of events leading to your membership in the group, or complicated in the sense that you don't want to tell me?"

Otto laughed. The guy was unreal. "A bit of both. Sorry."

"Sorry for what? You don't need to apologize to me for not sharing personal information, or is it rude now with everyone on the Internet not to share everything? I must say I'm a bit out of date. Perhaps you joined because of Vivian? She's quite an attractive girl."

"Me and Vivian? No. There's nothing there. I'd never make a play for her."

"Then you're a damn fool. If I was your age, I would have gotten a yes or a slap in the face weeks ago."

Smith nudged him in the ribs with a bony elbow. Otto stared at him incredulously. It always weirded him out when old people talked like that.

"I have a girlfriend."

"Ah, a gentleman! I'm glad to see they still exist. Turn in here. Yes, up to the house there and park right in front."

Dr. Smith's house was set back on a dirt road at the base of the Tucson Mountains just to the west of town. A screen of cacti and agave cut off the view from outside. More plants were scattered around the large yard, and a rambling bungalow stood in the center. Otto parked the car where he was told, and Grunt, who was driving the other car, parked behind them.

Dr. Smith ushered them into a rambling ranch house and invited them into the living room. One wall was entirely glass, and Otto bet that in daylight, the professor had an amazing view of the desert. The other three walls were adorned with Mexican religious paintings of Jesus, Mary, and the saints. Otto strolled around appreciating the art as Dr. Smith closed the curtains on the glass wall.

Dr. Smith came up to him and put a hand on his shoulder. "Like them?"

"They're nice, yeah."

"I've been a Roman Catholic all my life. No reason science and religion have to lock horns. Did you know that the percentage of devout scientists is the same as the general population? You don't hear that in the media much."

"Is all your religious art Mexican?" Otto asked.

Dr. Smith nodded. "That's the faith of this region, so that's what I follow. Who's to say that the Virgin Mary didn't look like a sad-eyed Mexican mother like in this icon here? And look at Jesus, he's a dead ringer for my pool cleaner."

Otto laughed. Dr. Smith smiled and continued.

"When Jesus comes back, he might work as a pool cleaner. It's a good humble job, and it would give him ample opportunity to spread the Word to the rich."

Dr. Yamazaki came up. "Maybe Jesus will come back as a woman. She could be a manicurist, preaching to millionaire ladies over the nail bath."

Dr. Smith shrugged. "Maybe. Or maybe he's already here working his old job of carpentry on one of these housing developments that are popping up all over the place."

Dr. Yamazaki wrinkled her nose. "He'd never destroy the desert like that. Anyway, we didn't come here for one of our endless debates on theology"—both scientists chuckled at the private joke—"we came here to discuss the Atlanteans."

"Ah yes, your life's work. Everyone, please sit." Dr. Smith gestured toward several leather chairs and a big sofa, all set around a coffee table. He turned to Dr. Yamazaki. "Now if I recall, it was your turn to bring the bottle, but considering the circumstances, let's give you a reprieve until next time."

Dr. Smith opened a small cabinet next to the sofa and pulled out a bottle of whiskey.

"Scapa, aged ten years. A fine Scotch from the Orkney Islands. The ten-year is actually better than the fifteen. Fifteen years ago, they were just restarting the old distillery after a hiatus and were only producing a great whiskey instead of an excellent one. Who wants a shot?"

Otto passed. Dr. Yuhle looked a bit red faced from his margarita and eagerly accepted a double, as did Otto and Dr. Yamazaki. Vivian had a single. Dr. Smith poured himself a generous amount.

The aged professor eased himself into an armchair, took a slow sip of his whiskey, and addressed the gathering.

"Scientific discoveries are generally built upon earlier work by other scientists, and that is the case with Akiko's—I mean Dr. Yamazaki's—discovery of the Atlantis gene. And that's no insult to a fine scientist. Television was developed by several different people simultaneously in both America and England, but it took Philo T. Farnsworth to make it practical. Same with Edison and the lightbulb. A Russian scientist named Alexander Lodygin actually invented it, and Edison made it commercially viable. Genetic researchers had noted that some apparently mixed-race people had an unusual set of genes, but no one before Yamazaki decided to investigate them."

"Why not?" Vivian asked before taking a sip of her whiskey.

Dr. Smith shrugged. "Racism. Since the genes weren't appearing in white subjects, it was assumed to be some cluster of genes from Africa or Asia, and no one bothered to investigate. The public likes to think that scientists are rational thinkers and above such things, but it isn't true. I've had to clean up my own mind."

Otto looked around at all the Hispanic art on the walls. "You don't seem very racist to me."

"You think not? When I was your age, I was killing Japanese soldiers on remote islands in the Pacific. Of course I didn't call them Japanese. I won't tell you what I called them. I hated them. I cheered when I read the news that the government had put all Japanese-Americans into internment camps. Good thing I had forty years to cool off after the war before Akiko here showed up at my office, asking for a research position."

"Admitting you're wrong is a sign of a true intellect," Dr. Yamazaki said, a serious look on her face.

Dr. Smith gave her a warm smile. "Perhaps. Anyway, we never took that set of genes seriously. You did. I've read all the reports you sent me via private courier, and I could see why you went for the cloak-and-dagger approach. The government would just love to get their hands on these people. There are elements in our military that want new weapons no matter what the cost."

Dr. Smith took a slow look around the room. "And that's what's happened, hasn't it? You're on the run, aren't you?"

Dr. Yamazaki blushed and said, "I can't really talk—"

The old professor silenced her with an upraised hand. "Don't tell me. It's best that I don't know. The real issue is finding out more about the Atlanteans, and I think I can help you with that. Since you sent me your findings, I've been running some computer simulations matched with legends about Atlantis to try to pin down their origins. I've come up with a few likely locations. If you want to find out more about the Atlanteans, and find more Atlanteans themselves, checking these areas would be a good idea."

Dr. Yamazaki leaned forward and eagerly asked, "Where do they come from?"

Dr. Smith smiled. "Don't let your enthusiasm cloud your judgment, Akiko. You know these findings are only probabilities based on insufficient data. But if you and I put our heads together, we might be able to narrow down the choices."

Smith turned to the others. "We are about to get quite technical, and I'm afraid you'll be bored listening to us. Feel free to have a look around the house. And you already know where the drinks cabinet is. Help yourself. I have quite a collection of Native American and Mexican art to enjoy, and a good library with more than genetics books. Also, if you're not afraid of the dark, you'll find an arroyo just behind the house. If you take a right, going toward the mountains, and follow the arroyo for about a quarter of a mile, you'll come to a side canyon on your right. Those of you interested in Southwestern lore will appreciate what you see there."

"What's there?" Otto asked.

Dr. Smith smiled. "Take a look and you tell me."

That piqued his curiosity. Otto looked around him. "Anyone up for a night hike?"

Grunt nodded. "Yeah, let's do it."

"Use only moonlight to find your way," Dr. Smith said.

Otto and Grunt looked at each other and shrugged.

"Anything you say," Otto said.

Vivian got up. "I'm going to make myself a daiquiri. Spending the past week picking sand out of my hair has made me thirsty."

They headed out of the room. It looked as though Vivian planned to stay and listen to the scientists talk. Otto wondered if she'd actually understand them or if she was being paranoid and wanted to catch every important conversation.

Grunt and Otto went out the back door and into the night. They soon found the back entrance to the yard and skittered down a rocky slope into an arroyo, a dry riverbed that was about ten feet wide. To the east, they could see the lights of Tucson. High above shone the gibbous moon, a few days from being full. To the west, the arroyo led into the darkness. A starry sky silhouetted black peaks. The only sound was the chirping of cicadas and a distant, mournful howl.

Otto stopped. "Was that a coyote?"

"Yeah," Grunt said, chuckling. "You're a city boy, I see. Don't worry. Coyotes are scavengers. They never attack people. I got my nine millimeter just in case."

They headed down the quiet arroyo, their boots crunching the gritty sand. The moonlight lit up the sand to make a gleaming, bone-white highway through the darkness. Occasionally they had to duck to avoid the branch of a mesquite tree or saguaro cactus, or step around some agave plant sticking out of the sand like a cluster of knives, but otherwise their way was clear. To either side, all was darkness, but Otto could see a large hill or ridge blotting out the stars ahead.

Grunt walked without a sound, confident and at ease. He was right. Otto was a city boy, and except for a few camping trips, he'd never spent much time in the outdoors. The stillness of the desert and the intermittent call of the coyote, which sounded closer now, unnerved him.

Otto spotted an opening in the bushes and cacti to their right. Beyond and above loomed a cliff face about a hundred yards away.

"Is that it?" Otto asked, the silence of the place making him keep his voice at a whisper.

"You got a good eye, Pyro," Grunt said. "We'll make a decent soldier out of you yet."

"I don't want to be a soldier."

"That's too bad, because you already are one."

The gap led to a smaller side arroyo about three feet wide. Otto imagined that during the big rainstorms Arizona got in August and September, it would be a fast-flowing stream, and the arroyo they had just left would be a raging river. He suspected they dried out as soon as the rain stopped, though. There sure wasn't any water there then.

The moon lit their way, making the sand of the dry streambed glow a pale white. It shone on the rocks that were closing in on them too, the way getting narrower as they penetrated into a small side canyon.

After a couple of minutes, the way opened up, and they saw that they stood at the dead end of a little box canyon. A cleft in the rock showed where the water fell down, and just to the side of that, Otto saw something that made him stop and stare.

It may have been the play of the light on the rock, the mixture of moonbeams and shadow, but the cliff looked like the giant, craggy face of an old Native American.

A long, slow exhalation from Grunt told Otto that he'd seen it too. It was so clear. Two rounded, seamed boulders formed the temples, a full ten feet across, with cavities below for eyes. Smaller rocks made up the cheeks and ears, and a horizontal crack above a sharp, jutting stone gave the impression of a mouth and chin.

For a minute, neither of them said anything. When Otto finally spoke, it was in hushed tones, as if he was in church.

"You should show this to Jim Running Horse."

"He knows about it," Grunt said, not taking his eyes off the beautiful image the moon and rocks had made.

"He told you about this?"

"No, but he knows about it."

They stared at it for a while longer. The vision sent chills up Otto's spine, not from fear but from an eerie realization that the history of the region had somehow been naturally inscribed onto the rock. It seemed unreal, but there it was.

"I once saw a book," Grunt said, keeping his voice low, "of ancient sacred sites in England. You know, stone circles and stuff like that. All pretty cool, but what was really interesting were some photos of trees and naturally shaped rocks near these sites. So many of them had animal or human shapes. There was this one tree that was a dead ringer for a druid's face. You could see the eyes and beard and hair and everything."

"Just like this."

"When old ways last long enough, they get imprinted on the land," Grunt said.

Otto nodded. It was just what he'd been figuring. He thought for a moment and then said, "Dr. Yamazaki says the Atlanteans have been around for thousands of years and spread all over the earth. Why haven't they been inscribed on the land?"

Grunt put a hand on his shoulder. "Dunno, Pyro. Maybe the signs are all around us, and we just don't know how to see them."

Chapter 12

JUNE 28, 2016, LANGLEY AIR
FORCE BASE, VIRGINIA

11:45 AM

General Meade and General Corbin strolled along a circular running track at Langley Air Force Base. No one was using it at the moment, and they could speak freely without fear of being overheard. The regular troops were all going about their duties, and the new recruits were off training elsewhere, or perhaps observing the artillery practice that Meade could hear booming in the distance. A light rain fell, but the two men didn't dare have their conversation inside. Even the office of a general could be wiretapped.

The government spied on itself as much as it spied on the people.

Meade admired Corbin's caution. He was a man after his own heart. They had already exchanged memory sticks containing their latest findings so nothing could be tracked of their activities online.

"What I don't understand," Meade said, "is why the aliens reveal themselves to us. If they're advanced enough to make an interstellar journey, surely they have the technology to hide from us. Our own military is already experimenting with an invisibility cloak. That must seem like medieval technology to them. Hell, with most of the nighttime sightings, all they'd have to do is turn their lights off. It's like they want us to know they're coming."

General Corbin nodded. "There's a theory that the aliens are preparing us for their visit, gradually getting the people of Earth used to the idea of their existence, so it won't be so much of a shock when they finally make contact."

"I've heard that theory too. Most people who suggest that think the extraterrestrials are friendly and are coming here to take us into some new age of wisdom and harmony, but the search patterns of the UFOs over military bases and other important spots prove they're planning an invasion. So why are they revealing themselves?"

Corbin shrugged, the rain dripping off the brim of his hat.

"It's strange, I agree. We're dealing with an alien intelligence here, or actually several alien races judging from the evidence, so it's difficult to tell what they might be thinking. One possibility is that they're playing a double game, that the optimists are half right. The aliens might reveal themselves to us, act like they're here to help, and then hit us unawares."

Meade rubbed his jaw. "Yeah. They could even recruit some humans to their side. Divide and conquer."

"Another possibility is that they want to test our response," General Corbin went on as they continued walking around the track. "It could be a kind of psychology experiment. See how quickly we accustom ourselves to their presence, and what we do about it. They could be so confident of their technological superiority that they don't need to worry about broadcasting their intentions. It's like a cat playing with a mouse before biting its head off."

"We're just going to have to be the mouse that bites back," Meade said.

"You mentioned that you're training one of the Atlanteans."

"Orion. Yes, he's quite a specimen," Meade said with pride. "If we had a regiment like him, we would never have to worry about a terrestrial enemy ever again. The problem is that we don't know what kind of weapons the aliens have."

"Actually, we do."

Meade turned to him. They stopped and faced one another. The nearest people were a group of soldiers marching on a road almost half a mile away. Even so, General Corbin lowered his voice as he spoke.

"I have access to some information you don't."

Meade nodded. Corbin was a four-star general, one of the highest-ranking military leaders in the country. Meade himself was only a one-star general, which made him feel as if he had won a bronze medal in the Olympics. That was impressive enough to the common rabble, but really all it meant was that he was a leader among the losers.

"What's this information?" Meade asked, hearing his voice come out breathless. The whole conversation had been like a dream come true. Finally he was getting some straight answers to a lifetime of questions.

Corbin looked around again before answering. "I've seen reports on the UFO that crashed in Roswell, reports that people at your level aren't allowed to know even exist. The consensus among our scientists is that the Roswell craft was simply a scout craft, not a main war vessel. Even so, it had lasers far in advance of anything we can replicate. In fact, the American 'invention' of lasers actually came about thanks to engineers analyzing the laser cannon on that craft and reverse-engineering it. Our lasers are barely one percent of the power of that thing, and that's because the Roswell laser cannon is made from material not found on this planet. The ship also had a disintegration ray, but the engineers haven't figured it out yet. It got badly mangled in the crash. The craft was highly armored too, and with an incredible maneuverability. Most air-to-air missiles would barely dent it, assuming they could hit it in the first place. So that scout vessel that crashed near Roswell back in 1947 could shoot down half our Air Force before we could take it out. Think what one of their warships could do!"

"Plus they've had half a century of technological advancement since then, just like we have," Meade grumbled, shaking his head. The whole thing looked hopeless. He looked out at the base, one of the biggest in the United States. Artillery boomed in the distance. The latest models of cannon could flatten a building in one hit. To the aliens, they'd seem like water pistols.

"We've seen evidence that they have advanced." Corbin nodded. "I'm sure you're aware of the wave of sightings of triangular UFOs over Belgium back in 1989 and 1990."

"You were stationed there at that time. What do you know?" Meade asked eagerly. Very little had been revealed about those sightings except vague and hysterical stories in the press.

"Not much more than you, except for something vital that never got out beyond some high-ranking officials in Belgium and the US. During one of the sightings, we scrambled six teams of F-16s to intercept. This was standard procedure because we wanted to get a closer look. Usually the UFOs just zipped away before we could get close, but this time one of the craft appeared directly between a Belgian base and two of our own bases. The Belgians sent up some of their guys, and we sent up some too. The craft had nowhere to go, and we managed to get closer than ever before. Too close, it turned out. One of the American pilots got overeager and made directly for the craft, powering his afterburners for all they were worth. He was still more than two miles away when the UFO fired a disintegration ray. The F-16 turned into a cloud of atoms."

Corbin fell silent, his face grim. Meade thought of the young man who had been piloting that jet fighter. He'd given his life to protect his country, his planet. They owed it to him to make sure the planet stayed protected. Finally Corbin spoke.

"Our engineers estimate that the range of the disintegration ray on the Roswell craft couldn't have been more than one mile. Something to do with power requirements and the nature of the beam. I'm afraid I don't understand all the technical details. The ray the UFO over Belgium used went twice that distance."

Meade shook his head. "Even if we had an entire army of Atlanteans, I don't see how we can defeat them. All they have to do is stay out of reach and blast us."

Corbin met his eye. "So what does a military commander do when he's hopelessly outgunned?"

Meade felt as if he was back in a strategy class at West Point.

"Trickery. Guerrilla warfare." Meade snapped his fingers. "We make contact! If the aliens are looking for traitors to help with their invasion, we can pretend to be those traitors. We get them in close and then hit them with all we got!"

General Corbin smiled and put a hand on Meade's shoulder. "Exactly."

"But how do we make contact?"

Corbin inclined his head. "That's the problem. So far as we know, the aliens have never tried to get in touch. All the accounts of alien contact and abduction seem to be by lunatics or hucksters trying to sell books. I set up a team to investigate every single claim we could trace, and not one turned out to be legitimate. Also, the writing we've found in the Roswell wreck has never been deciphered. Even if we could get them to talk to us, we couldn't make ourselves understood."

"They might solve that problem for us," Meade said. "I'm sure they've been listening in to our communications. It's easy enough even with our level of technology. They must be able to speak all the major Earth languages. Archaeologists decipher ancient languages with far less to work with. They must have a computer that can speak English as good as you or I. We just have to get them to talk with us."

"You're right. I've been dealing with this stuff in isolation for so long that my thinking has become narrow. Thank God I've finally found another man to trade ideas with."

"Are there any other generals we can trust?" Meade asked. He realized he was already committing himself to the plan. Of course, a general contacting a foreign power without orders from the president could be considered treason, but he and Corbin had already committed treason when they exchanged information about their secret projects. They had gone too far to turn back.

Corbin thought for a moment. "There are a few we might be able to talk to, but that would be risky. Let me feel them out a bit. In the meantime, let's just stick with each other. I've spent years assembling a staff of junior officers I can trust, and I'm sure you've done the same. First thing we have to do is accelerate the training of this Orion fellow. Do you have any others you can train?"

Meade nodded. "Several. Plus there's a teenage girl who has lots of potential. She's already being manipulated by two of my best agents. She'll be ready soon enough. Once she is, we'll bring her in, work on her with drugs and a hypnotist I have on the payroll, and get her ready. We'll make her disappear. It happens to kids all the time. No one will suspect anything. She's got some interesting powers beyond the physical ones. She could be the best soldier we have."

Chapter 13

JUNE 28, 2016, TUCSON, ARIZONA

10:30 PM

Otto and Grunt returned to Dr. Smith's house to find him, Yuhle, and Dr. Yamazaki studying several large maps spread over the coffee table. As they entered, Vivian called out from a chair in the corner, "Hey, boys, ready to go on vacation?"

Otto thought she sounded a bit drunk.

Grunt laughed. "When was the last time either of us had one of those?"

"No, I'm serious," Vivian said. "The professor here says that if we are going to find the Atlanteans, we'll have to go on a world tour. Maybe this mission will finally get us somewhere with nightlife."

Dr. Smith looked up from the map. "A world tour? No. More like a stop in two or three likely spots. We've looked at concentrations of the Atlantis gene correlated with likely traditions of the location of Atlantis."

"I thought Atlantis sank," Otto said.

"In most traditions, including the famous Greek one, it did, but not in all stories. Some say Atlantis was on land that still exists and got wiped out in a natural disaster or invasion. Even if it was on an island that sank, the nearest existing land would be a good place to look."

"Where's the most likely place?" Grunt asked.

"Morocco."

Grunt's face clouded, and his face turned red. Otto unconsciously took a step away from him.

"Why Morocco?" Grunt demanded.

Dr. Smith pointed to the map, seemingly unaware of Grunt's reaction. "Northwest Africa is the most likely spot for the Atlanteans to have originated. Several scholars during the Renaissance looked at ancient texts and found that Atlantis may have been just off the Atlantic coast of Morocco. When it sank, the Atlanteans would most likely have come ashore there. The population in that region has always been mixed, with Arabs, Berbers, Europeans, and black Africans all mingling. The Atlanteans would fit right in."

Grunt scowled and walked out. Vivian got a worried look on her face and hurried after him. Otto glanced at the two curiously and then sat down on the sofa to study the map.

"Where else could they be?" he asked.

Dr. Smith's finger traced a route down the west coast of Africa.

"Farther south, just off the shore of Gambia, and also on the islands on the eastern fringe of the Caribbean," he said. "Morocco looks like the most promising start, though."

"Why?" Otto asked.

"Several researchers and ancient travelers put it there. A historian named D. A. Godron wrote a book all the way back in 1868 claiming Atlantis was in the western Sahara, what's now the southern part of Morocco or perhaps northern Mali. Maybe the fabled city of Timbuktu is a remnant of that civilization. A more detailed account comes from Félix Berlioux, who in 1874 wrote a book titled *Les Atlantes: Histoire de l'Atlantis et de l'Atlas Primitif.* That translates to *The Atlanteans: History of Atlantis and the Primitive Atlas Mountains.*"

"When did you start reading French?" Dr. Yamazaki asked.

Dr. Smith smiled at her. "Have to do something with my retirement. Anyway, Berlioux traveled all over northwest Africa. He found evidence that Atlantis was once situated where the Atlas Mountains slope down into the Atlantic Ocean. There are a number of archaeological sites between Casablanca and Agadir that show signs of great age and sophistication. He claims the Atlanteans ruled over a great empire in North Africa but were eventually defeated by the Egyptians and Phoenicians in the thirteenth century BC. One interesting thing he noticed was that many people in that region have brilliant blue eyes despite having otherwise African features. He theorized that the Atlanteans looked like Scandinavians and mingled with the black Africans to create these blue-eyed dark people."

"We know better," Otto said.

"Yes," Dr. Yamazaki said, nodding eagerly, "the Atlanteans have a mixture of features, but a Frenchman in the nineteenth century would have still been thinking along the old racial lines. A lot of European researchers thought the Atlanteans were white simply because they couldn't conceive of any other race having an advanced civilization."

"So what about Gambia and the Caribbean?" Otto asked. "From what I've read, there's plenty linking the Caribbean to Atlantis. There's some huge ancient ruins on some of the islands, and even more underwater just off shore. It's pretty cool."

Dr. Jones nodded. "Yes, those are interesting. There's no proof they're ancient, though. And many geologists say those underwater ruins are simply natural formations. But the Caribbean is close to where many accounts put Atlantis, so it's a candidate."

"What about Gambia?" Otto asked, looking at the unfamiliar country. It was on the west coast of Africa, a little strip of land on either side of a big river.

"Gambia is a possibility thanks to one of the oldest accounts of Atlantis," Dr. Smith said. "Around 500 BC, an admiral from Carthage took a voyage down the west coast of Africa."

"Carthage? Where's that?" Otto asked.

Dr. Smith sighed. "I see kids aren't getting any classical education these days. Carthage was a powerful kingdom in what is now Tunisia in North Africa. Their capital city was founded by the Phoenicians, the greatest explorers of the ancient world. The Carthaginians even fought off the Roman Empire for many years and dominated the Mediterranean. This admiral, who was named Hanno, wrote about his voyage, and his story has been preserved until modern times. Hanno talks about reaching an island called Kernë, which many scholars associate with Atlantis, at the mouth of the River Gambia on the west coast of Africa. The ancient civilization was long gone even in Hanno's day, but the island remained a center for trade between foreign ships and the local natives."

Dr. Yamazaki studied the map again. "So I guess in order of likelihood, Morocco is our best bet, followed by Gambia and then the Caribbean."

Dr. Yuhle chuckled. "Then I guess we're going to Morocco. I've always wanted to see Africa."

Otto looked at Yuhle. "We can't go anywhere until we get Jaxon out of trouble."

Yuhle raised a reassuring hand. "We won't leave her behind. It's why we sprang you, remember? You're the only one of us she knows and trusts. So the first thing to do is plan how we can get her out of there without putting her in worse danger than she's already in. Once we have her, we can get out of the country. We had been talking about doing that anyway. We need to get out of General Meade's reach."

Otto's heart raced. He might see Jaxon soon! What would he say to her? Would she still want to date him? Otto brushed that thought away. The first thing to do was make sure she was safe, and Edward had said General Meade had put her in a house with two deadly agents. Getting her free without any of the team getting killed would be tricky. He could worry about Jaxon's feelings for him later.

The scientists had gone back to talking about genetics and archaeology. Their conversation became increasingly technical, and soon Otto was lost, so he got up to follow Vivian and Grunt. He needed to know what was wrong and get it fixed. The mercenaries were their best chance at saving Jaxon.

He found them in the front hall, angrily whispering to each other. Grunt's face was contorted with rage, and he was violently shaking his head. Vivian was talking to him in soothing tones, stroking his muscular arm like a mother comforting an oversized child.

"What's going on?" Otto asked.

"I ain't going," Grunt declared.

"Why not?" Otto asked.

"None of your damn business, but I ain't going."

"We finally have a clue to this mystery, and now you want to bail?" Otto couldn't believe it.

"Yeah, I'm gonna bail."

"We have to get Jaxon first!"

Grunt nodded. "We will. I'll help. After that, I'm out."

Vivian stroked his arm again. "Honey, don't say that, I—"

"Don't 'honey' me. I said no, and you know I mean it."

Vivian hung her head. "Yeah, I know you mean it."

Otto threw his hands in the air. "But why?"

Grunt glowered at him. "Did you miss the part where I said it was none of your damn business?"

Otto felt something harden inside his chest. He glared back at Grunt. "It's my damn business if you're going to endanger the Atlantis Allegiance and my girlfriend. We need you."

Grunt's face got even redder than it was before, and for a moment, Otto thought he might lash out. After a few seconds, Grunt visibly controlled himself and replied, "I've been to Morocco before, back when I was living life way differently than I am now. I've been all over North

Africa, in fact, doing things I ain't proud of. I'm not going back to the scene of the crime."

Crime? Otto thought. He wanted to ask, but Grunt didn't look as though he was going to say any more than he already had. He took a deep breath and said, "Look, both of you have dropped hints that you did some dirty work before you came clean. I don't care. The past is the past. We need—"

"What the hell do you know about it?" Grunt bellowed as Vivian restrained him. "You think the past just conveniently goes away? Tell that to the people we..."

Grunt's voice trailed off. He turned and stalked out of the room, muttering "dumb kid" under his breath.

Otto was surprised to see Vivian didn't follow. Instead she stood there, brushing at her eyes.

"You okay?" Otto asked.

"No, I'm not."

"You coming with us to Morocco?"

Vivian paused and took a deep breath. "Yes."

Otto looked over his shoulder in the direction where Grunt had disappeared.

"So what's wrong with—"

"Don't ask." Vivian shook her head and walked off.

When Otto returned to the living room, he found everyone packing up to leave. Dr. Yamazaki gave the old scientist a hug.

"Thank you for all your help. You take care of yourself, you hear me?"

Dr. Smith chuckled. "It looks like you're the one who should worry."

Dr. Yamazaki's face clouded. "I feel like I've been drafted into a war. At least I'm on the right side."

Dr. Smith shook his head. "It's never as clear-cut as that, as you well know."

As the others started filing out of the room and to the driveway, Dr. Smith put a hand on Otto's shoulder. He held out a gold chain and medallion. "Take my St. Christopher."

Otto blinked. It was the same one he had noticed hanging from Dr. Smith's rearview mirror. "Are you sure?"

The professor grinned. "He's the patron saint of travelers. My mother gave it to me when I was on my first big trip, to the Pacific in 1944."

"Your mother gave this to you when you went off to World War Two? I can't take this."

Dr. Smith chuckled, deep laugh lines creasing his face. "Sure you can. You'll be traveling more than I will."

Otto put it around his neck, feeling a bit embarrassed. "Well, if you want, but I'm not really big into saints and stuff."

"That's okay. They're big into you."

Otto didn't know what to say to that. Dr. Smith extended a hand. Otto shook it.

"Good luck, and I hope you find that girlfriend of yours," the old man said.

"Finding her isn't the problem, saving her is. I hope I'm man enough for that."

"Well, if you can live with a woman like Vivian and still think about your girlfriend, you're a better man than me."

Otto rolled his eyes. The guy was old enough to be his grandfather, or even his great-grandfather.

Dr. Smith grinned. "What I mean to say is, I think you have every chance of saving her. The real fight will be after that. I've seen the government do a lot of bad things in my time. When the military did atomic tests in the Marshall Islands in the forties and fifties, they knew the wind would blow the radiation onto neighboring islands. They didn't mind, because then they could study the effects on the islanders. A decade before that, they told a group of black men with syphilis that they were being given a new type of medication. It was a placebo, nothing but sugar and water. Really they just wanted to see what would happen if the patients were left untreated. The worst of their dirty tricks are reserved for minorities and foreigners, but they'll hurt white Americans, too, if it gets them what they want. Don't think your privileged background makes you immune. There are elements in this government that don't care a fig about us, but mostly the people who make up this great country, even in the government, are decent folk. It's important to remember that."

Otto grimaced. "I haven't been seeing many decent folk in this country lately."

Dr. Smith cocked his head. "Really? You need to look harder. You're like a fish, cursing the ocean because it contains sharks."

The old man took the St. Christopher out of Otto's hand and put it around Otto's neck. "I pray this protects you. Look for the good no matter how much bad you see, and I think you'll be all right. Now go find that girl of yours."

Otto nodded, too moved to speak, and went out to join the rest of the Atlantis Allegiance.

Chapter 14

JUNE 29, 2016, LOS ANGELES,
CALIFORNIA

6:00 PM

"So, how are those newspaper assignments going?" Isadore asked.

It was dinnertime, and Jaxon sat with her foster parents in their sleek, modern dining room. The walls were all spotlessly white. No pictures hung on them because, as they explained, "it distracts from the conversation."

In the center stood a long table of heavy, worn oak. The centerpiece was a bronze sculpture consisting of big globes attached by little rods and a couple of spikes sticking out. A shiny brass plate on the base revealed it was called "Consciousness Rising IV."

The only other decorations in the room were four neatly pruned potted plants, all standing in identical white pots in each corner of the room. For some reason, they reminded Jaxon of her geometry class, where Mr. Wilson always kept giving examples from chess. Jaxon felt as if she was being checkmated by ferns.

She giggled a little as she took another bite of salad. *What a weird thought. This place is driving me crazy.*

As if her life wasn't crazy enough already. Cokehead classmates, painted grass, and then a secret life wandering the streets in the dead of night.

It was the city, not just the house. At first she thought both were boring, but suddenly everything seemed full of possibility. Los Angeles had finally become interesting.

She took another bite of salad. Was she forgetting something?

"Jaxon? Hellooooooo," Stephen said.

Jaxon perked up. "Hmmm?"

"Isadore asked you a question."

"Oh yeah!" Jaxon turned to her foster mother and nodded. "Sure. That's fine."

A flicker of annoyance passed over Isadore's face. "It wasn't a yes or no question. I was asking how those newspaper assignments were going."

"Oh, fine. She's giving them to us every week."

"How is it going with the dyslexia?"

Jaxon shrugged and shoveled more food in her mouth. She didn't want to talk about it. "It takes a bit longer to get things done."

"Don't talk with your mouth full. It's unladylike. I noticed you picked an interesting topic."

Jaxon looked up at Isadore. She had been reading her papers? It would have been nice if she'd asked first. Just because Jaxon had to write them on Isadore's spare laptop didn't mean that she could read anything she wanted.

A cold wave of worry passed through her. She had been writing about the teenaged vigilante for the past three weeks. It seemed as though there was a new story about him almost every day. Since she'd learned the vigilante was

Brett, she'd been tracking everything the press said about him. The day before, the teacher had asked for volunteers to read their papers. Though embarrassed by her dyslexia and bad reading skills, she couldn't resist the temptation to put her hand up. Although Courtney and some of the others did their usual snickering, watching Brett squirm in the back row, trying to hide his embarrassment, had been worth it.

But had she been too obvious about the whole thing? She'd been sneaking out most nights. What if Stephen and Isadore caught her? What if they put two and two together?

She realized she needed to say something. Fast.

"Yeah, well, it's kinda interesting, you know? Growing up in so many group homes, I met a lot of problem kids, kids who had been in trouble with the law and stuff. This guy is taking that whole rebel thing and turning it around."

"Don't you think it's a bit dangerous?" Isadore asked.

"Sure, but he's good at martial arts, so he can get away with it," she replied, quickly adding, "That's what the papers say, anyway."

Isadore shook her head. "Being good at martial arts isn't always enough. If that young man comes up against someone with a gun, he could wind up dead."

Jaxon shifted in her seat. That was something she had been worried about. She and Brett had talked about it, and Brett had said that even though his dad had a pistol in the house, he didn't want to bring it along. He was afraid having a gun would make other people quicker to use theirs, and he wasn't sure he could shoot someone anyway.

"Yeah, I guess he could," Jaxon murmured.

Stephen took a sip of wine and asked, "Do you think what he's doing is right?"

Jaxon hadn't really given it much thought. "Yeah. I mean, yeah, he's probably breaking some laws, but he's helping people too. The police can't be everywhere."

"Certainly not in LA," Isadore grumbled. "My car has been broken into twice."

Stephen inclined his head. "But if doing the right thing even if it's illegal and dangerous is morally acceptable, then where does that leave the rule of law?"

Jaxon almost groaned out loud. She sensed another of Stephen and Isadore's philosophical dinners coming up. Last night it had been "What's More Important: Security Or Democracy?" The night before that, it was "Is Human Testing Justified If It Saves Lives?" Most of those discussions were more like lectures, with them doing the lecturing and her doing the listening.

But before the lecture, she always had to give her opinion.

"I dunno," Jaxon said with a shrug.

Her foster parents weren't going to let her off that easy.

"But what do you think?" Stephen persisted. "Is it okay to break a law if it helps society?"

"Um, sure, I guess."

"But how do you decide if you're right or wrong?" Isadore asked.

Jaxon sighed. Couldn't she just eat her dinner in peace?

"I don't know. I guess it's obvious sometimes. Like during Civil Rights when black people marched against segregation. They broke a bad law so it would get changed. And then there are the people in the Middle East protesting against dictatorships. They're doing the right thing."

"Yes, but who gets to decide?"

Jaxon suppressed a groan. It looked as though the conversation was going to go on for a while.

"I guess you have to decide for yourself," Jaxon said. "And if you're wrong, then it's your responsibility."

Isadore took a sip from her wine and asked, "So everyone just gets to decide whether to follow the law or not?"

"Doesn't everyone make that decision anyway? Sure, most people choose to follow the law, but sometimes the law isn't strong enough to protect people, and you have to take things into your own hands."

She hadn't really thought about it much before. She had been going out at night for the excitement, but she had discovered that when she helped someone, she always felt as though she had made a difference. She'd been bullied so much, ignored and kicked around so much, that she felt good protecting someone in the same situation.

Smacking someone who really, really deserved it was a plus too.

Especially those guys attacking that prostitute just down the block. It still sent chills down her spine to remember that woman talking about being in a group home. She wondered how many of the girls she'd met in the system would end up like that.

Stephen and Isadore gave each other a look and nodded. Jaxon prepared for the lecture. They would talk and talk, and her eyes would glaze over, and she would nod automatically until they stopped. It was always the same.

Not that evening. Strangely, they returned to their meal and didn't say a word.

At midnight, Jaxon slipped out as usual. If Brett hadn't been waiting for her, she wouldn't have gone at all, because her foster parents' conversation had made her nervous, but she had been too flustered to make up an excuse to use her cell phone. She could have always said she needed to check an assignment with another student, but she didn't trust herself to say that without shaking and stammering.

Once she was vaulting out of her window, she felt an extra thrill at the risk she was taking. As her fingers left the windowsill behind and she launched herself through the air, on instinct she tucked into a roll, did a somersault, and landed on her feet in the yard.

She blinked and looked down at herself in wonder. She'd never learned to do that. It had just come naturally. Grinning from ear to ear, she sprinted through the backyard, over the fence, and into the residential area behind the Grants' home.

As she strolled down the dimly lit sidewalk, passing little patches of front lawn, she let the quiet of the night envelop her. It was so peaceful out there. It was strange, because she shouldn't feel at peace at all. She was a teenage girl walking alone in the middle of the night along an empty street. She was inviting trouble. In fact, she actually wanted to find it. So why should that be the most relaxing part of her day?

Because everything was clear. There she didn't have to fit into anyone's mold. She didn't have to take anyone's trash talking. All she had to do was deal with dangerous people, people who wanted to hurt her or someone else. Bad guys versus good girl, with no rules and no one watching. That made things a lot simpler.

Jaxon shook her head as she looked at all the brown patches of dead grass in front of the homes. California's drought had gotten so bad no one was allowed to water their lawns anymore, and the people who lived in that neighborhood couldn't afford to paint their grass green.

Then she had an idea. She checked her watch. It was a bit early to meet Brett. She had some time to kill.

Jaxon stopped and took a step to the edge of the nearest lawn. Peering at the darkened house a moment to make sure no one was watching, she crouched down and placed her hand on the dry, crackly grass.

She felt a tingling in her palm and all her fingers. She relaxed, focusing on her hand and imagining life coming back to the grass. After a moment, she pulled away her hand and gasped.

It had worked. The brown grass was marked by a green patch in the shape of her hand. She touched it and found it smooth and lush.

For a minute, she did nothing but stare, her mind empty of thoughts.

She walked down the street for a little while, her mind filled with wonder. It was a miracle she was witnessing, and she had performed it. On impulse, she went to another lawn and tried again.

Again she left a handprint of green grass where all the other grass was brown and dead.

Wait, dead? Jaxon wondered. Was she actually bringing plants back to life? That sounded impossible, but then again, what she was already doing was impossible. Perhaps the grass wasn't really dead, just in hibernation until more rain fell? She didn't know enough about plants to say. She'd have to ask Stephen.

By the time she made it to the rendez-vous with Brett, a dozen green handprints decorated the lawns of the neighborhood between her house and the highway.

Brett was waiting in his Porsche on an access road to the highway. He waved as she came into the beams of his headlights, and he opened the door for her.

"Aha! The superhero welcomes his sidekick," he said in a voice that sounded as though it belonged on some cartoon.

"I'm not your sidekick."

"I was just kidding. I would never call my girlfriend my sidekick. I'm a feminist, you know."

"Yeah, sure you are. Reality check: I'm not your girlfriend."

"Oh, come on! I've put in the time."

Jaxon rolled her eyes. "Are we going to go fight evil, or am I going to have to smack you?"

Brett revved the car and peeled out onto the access ramp.

"This car Daddy bought you isn't going to change my mind," Jaxon said, buckling her seat belt. She didn't trust Brett's driving.

"Maybe not, but it's going to get us to a crappy neighborhood where we can have some fun and get into the papers again. Hey, did you read the late edition?"

"No."

"We're in it for that carjacker we grabbed down on Florence. Look it up. The headline is 'Mystery Teen Superhero gets Female Sidekick.'"

"Great, the newspaper reporter is as sexist as you are," Jaxon grumbled. Then she grew nervous. "Aren't you worried about getting caught?"

Brett shrugged. "Not before that girl live-streamed us."

"Did she get me too?" Jaxon asked, anxious.

"I'm not sure. I hope her phone didn't pick up you saying my name."

"Sorry about that."

"It's okay. You couldn't have known what she was doing."

"Damn, we really could be in trouble," Jaxon said. She chewed on her knuckle.

Brett grinned. "Nah, don't worry about it! They'll never connect us to that video or to the newspaper reports. It's not like reporters are watching beatingthebums. com. And the homeless guy isn't going to say anything. Who would listen to him?"

Suddenly Jaxon had a horrible thought. A chill went down her spine. "Maybe the press isn't looking at beatingthebums. com, but Courtney is."

Brett's face fell. "Uh-oh."

"What are we going to do?" Jaxon asked.

Brett's face went blank. "Uh…"

"Sorry, forgot you aren't the brains of this outfit."

Brett looked more surprised than insulted. "What do you mean? I think of lots of stuff."

"All right, then. Think of a way out of this mess."

Brett's forehead furrowed. It didn't look as though it furrowed very often. In fact, his forehead seemed to resist furrowing, as though that was something it wasn't designed to do. After a moment, his forehead stopped trying to furrow, and Brett shook his head.

"Nope, can't think of anything."

Jaxon sighed. "So what do we do?" she asked.

Brett shrugged. "Nothing we can do tonight. Look, I'll talk to Courtney. I'll tell her about the video—"

"Don't do that!"

"She'll find it anyway. That's one of her favorite websites right now. I'll tell her to keep quiet, or I'll go to the principal about the coke dealing."

Jaxon looked at him in amazement. "You'd do that?"

"Why not? I'd get in as much trouble as you would."

"Wow. You actually came up with a good plan all by yourself."

"I do it all for you, baby!"

Jaxon groaned and rolled her eyes. How could someone have such a cool double life and still be such a dork?

"I'm not a baby."

"Sorry. I'm trying."

"And failing."

"Oh, come on! I haven't tried to put my arm around you for a week now!"

"You don't earn brownie points for not harassing me. All you earn is the right to speak with me."

Brett drove in silence for a minute. Jaxon gave him a sidelong glance and saw him frowning, his lips moving silently as he tried to put his thoughts into words.

"Look," he said. "I'm sorry if I come off wrong, but I really like you. You're like no other girl in the school."

"Yeah, I've never had plastic surgery, and my brain isn't filled with cocaine."

Brett chuckled. "That's only part of it. You're different, you know? In a good way. If someone told me another person at school was doing these night adventures, I would have guessed it was you."

Jaxon didn't know what to say to that. The conversation lulled into silence again. That time, it was a comfortable silence.

They pulled off the highway onto a business loop. Run-down motels with flickering neon signs offered hourly rates. Women in fishnet stockings and imitation fur coats walked along the sidewalk, waving to passing drivers. In a parking lot were half a dozen cars in a little cluster. A group of men knocked back cheap booze and watched as two guys fought each other. Brett came to a stop at a red light. A man in shabby clothes staggered out into the street and walked up to the passenger-side door. Jaxon locked it as Brett checked for oncoming cars and then revved his Porsche through the red light.

"Ugh, how do you find these places?" Jaxon said, disgusted.

"It's amazing what people will talk about on the Internet. You just have to find the right chat room."

"My parents would kill me if they caught me looking at something like that," Jaxon said, feeling the old familiar ache when she said "parents." It was one lie she'd never gotten used to.

"So would mine, but it's not like they're going to check."

Jaxon looked at him. "Do they know you go out this late?"

"I don't know. Maybe. Mom will be on her fifth gin and tonic by now, and Dad, well, we might see Dad around here somewhere."

"Seriously?"

"Usually he goes for higher-priced call girls. He might decide to go slumming once in a while, though."

Jaxon felt a tug of pity for him. Otto's parents had been the same way. She couldn't decide which was worse—not having parents at all or being stuck with a pair of losers who didn't give a damn about their child.

Brett pulled off onto a dark side street and parked the Porsche. He turned to Jaxon. "So how do you want to handle this?" he asked.

Jaxon looked around the street, the adrenaline pumping in her veins. She didn't see anyone nearby. "Let's just go for a walk. Trouble will find us soon enough."

They got out and started to walk toward the main street where they had seen all the action. In the distance, they could hear drunken shouting. Brett edged away from Jaxon. After a moment, he crossed the street and walked parallel to her.

"Are you using me as bait?" Jaxon called over.

"This will attract them quicker. We can turn in early. Maybe I won't fall asleep in class tomorrow."

Jaxon chuckled and shook her head in disbelief, then laughed out loud when she realized that she didn't mind doing that at all. Yeah, bring them on!

They came to the main street and turned a corner. Brett cut across the four-lane road, leaving Jaxon very much alone. Up ahead, she could see the neon glow of the strip of cheap motels. A car came up the street and slowed. She saw the shadowy figure of a man at the wheel, staring at her. After a moment, the car picked up speed and passed her. She felt energy prickle through her entire body. Brett was right. It wouldn't take long.

It took even less time than they'd expected.

A loud beeping came from the street where they had parked. Brett sprinted across the street to join her.

"That's my car alarm!"

"Looks like you had more than one piece of bait," Jaxon said.

They hurried around the corner together. Up ahead, half a block away, the Porsche's lights flashed in time to the loud beeping. Two figures in hooded sweatshirts were busy prying off Brett's hubcaps, completely ignoring the car alarm.

As Brett and Jaxon ran for them, the thieves looked up, spotted them, and took off. One had a hubcap tucked under his arm.

Brett angled toward him. Jaxon grabbed his arm.

"Let them go."

"They have one of my hubcaps!"

"Forget it. These are small-timers. Let's not waste our time on them."

Brett looked at the fleeing figures uncertainly, then shrugged.

"I should have known something like this would happen."

"Ask your daddy to buy you a less expensive car."

"You kids all right?" someone drawled from behind them.

They turned and saw a skeletal man in baggy sweatpants and a grimy T-shirt. His face was sunken, with eyes that bugged out. Even in the dim glow of the flickering streetlight, Jaxon could see his eyes were glassy and bloodshot. The man sniffled and wiped his nose with the back of his hand.

"We're fine, thanks," Jaxon said, taking a step back and keeping an eye on him.

"You kids gotta be careful around here," the man slurred, wiping his nose again. Jaxon could barely hear him over the noise of the car alarm.

Brett edged closer to Jaxon. "Yeah, well, thanks for your concern. Bye."

The stranger turned unsteadily and looked at Brett's Porsche. "Nice wheels! Is that a 911 GT3?"

"You know your cars, buddy," Brett said in a friendly voice. "I need to turn off that car alarm before I wake the whole neighborhood. Bye."

"Can I take it for a spin?"

Brett's face hardened. "I don't think so."

The man cocked his head and studied him. "You think I'm not good enough to drive your car."

It came out as a statement, not a question.

"It's not that, man, I—"

"Shut up, rich kid. I've been working all my life, and I'll never be able to afford a car like this. What are you? Sixteen? And here you are with a Porsche 911 GT3!"

Brett took Jaxon by the arm, and they stepped away. Jaxon kept a close eye on the man, unsure how to handle that.

"Hey! I'm talking to you!"

He walked after them.

"Leave us alone," Brett said.

The man snarled, pulled a pistol out of his pocket, and aimed it at Brett's head.

For a moment, the three of them stood motionless, like some strange, menacing statue in the middle of the street. The car alarm rang in their ears.

"Give me the keys," the stranger said, wiping his nose with his free hand.

"Whoa, take it easy. I'm reaching in my pocket for my keys now," Brett said.

Jaxon was amazed at how calm he sounded. She was trembling all over. Her mind remained calm, calculating the distance between her and the gunman, thinking about the moves Marquis had taught her for just such a scenario, gauging whether the guy would let them go once he had the keys. He was a menace and needed to be taken down, whether he let them go or not. He had a gun, though. Was it worth the risk?

Isadore's words over dinner came back to her. "If that young man comes up against someone with a gun, he could wind up dead."

Brett extended his arm, the keys dangling from his hand. The gunman stepped forward to take them.

Should she make a move? She couldn't reach the gunman without stepping toward him, and that might make him pull the trigger. No, as long as he took only the Porsche, it was best to do nothing.

But what if Brett tried something stupid?

Jaxon tensed as the man grabbed the keys. To her immense relief, Brett let him. The gunman shivered all over, his bug eyes growing even bigger. He snuffled, wiped his nose with the back of his hand, and turned to Jaxon.

"Want to go for a ride, girl?" he said in a sickly sweet voice.

Rage rose up within her, followed quickly by fear. Not fear for herself. Fear for Brett.

As soon as the gunman said the words, Brett started edging toward him. Jaxon stepped to the side to make the gunman turn a little away from Brett. The guy was so fixated on her he didn't even notice Brett's movement.

Brett leaped for him. The sound made the gunman turn, bringing his pistol around in an attempt to gun Brett down.

Jaxon was quicker than both of them. She dove for the attacker and swept her hand under his wrist to make his gun hand jerk upward. The pistol barked as the bullet flew harmlessly toward the sky. Her other hand was already hitting hard on the pressure point on the back of his wrist.

Marquis had explained that she could stun a person using the move, that the pain would be so intense that the assailant wouldn't be able to use that hand for a couple of minutes.

Marquis didn't know about her strength. A bone snapped, and the man wailed. Jaxon performed a takedown and pinned him to the pavement. As the man fell, a small pipe and a clear plastic bag filled with some sort of little crystals fell onto the street.

"Damn, a meth head. That was a close one," Brett said. "You all right?"

"Yeah," she huffed.

Jaxon stood there for a moment, pressing the gunman down onto the ground, too afraid to let him go. She looked Brett over and found he was unhurt.

A police siren wailed in the distance, coming closer.

"There's actually a patrol car in this neighborhood?" Jaxon said.

"I'm surprised too. Let's get out of here before LA's finest show up."

Jaxon was afraid to let go of the gunman.

"What about him?" she asked.

Brett pulled a strip of looped plastic out of his pocket. With a quick movement, he brought the gunman's hands behind his back, put them through the loops, and bound them together.

"Zip cuffs," he explained. "Cheap and disposable, just like this guy."

Once their attacker was restrained, they leaped into the car, turned off the alarm, and zoomed away.

The car veered to the right. A telephone pole loomed up ahead.

"Watch out!" Jaxon cried, grabbing the wheel and swerving out of the way just in time.

The car wove along the lane, crossing the centerline. Brett was trembling all over. He turned a corner, nearly hitting a truck coming from the other direction, and downshifted, grinding gears. He struggled with the clutch for a moment, and the engine stalled. The Porsche slowed to a stop, the wheels rubbing against the curb.

"What happened?" Jaxon asked.

Brett didn't answer. He was leaning against the steering wheel, sobbing, his face in his hands.

Chapter 15

JUNE 29, 2016, ALBUQUERQUE, NEW MEXICO

NOON

General Meade returned to the Poseidon Project with a new sense of optimism. He'd finally found an ally. Not only that, he had in his possession the full data of General Corbin's decade of research. Together they could forge ahead and develop the Atlanteans to their full potential.

And then what? Meade felt troubled. America couldn't face the alien threat if the nation was led by a bunch of weak-willed politicians who only cared about getting reelected and pandering to the big donors who financed their campaigns.

That sort of legalized corruption was ruining the country. It was ruining the military too. Jobs that used to be performed by soldiers were handled by civilian contractors who had won fat deals with the government. That meant civilians on base, which was bad for security, and big inequalities in pay, which was bad for morale.

The head computer programmer for General Meade's own base used to be a man in uniform. When that man's enlistment was up, he became a civilian, got a job with the firm that was taking over the base's programming services, and ended up sitting at the same desk doing the same job as before but getting paid three times as much. How could they run an army like that?

No, the politicians had to go. It was the only way. Corbin agreed with him on that.

But to overthrow a democratically elected government, even a corrupt one... it went against everything he had sworn to uphold. It went against the reasons he'd put on a uniform in the first place.

It will only be temporary, he told himself. *Just until Earth is secure. It wouldn't be the first time a democratic nation suspended some legal rights in order to face down a dangerous enemy.*

Meade suppressed a shudder. He'd faced combat dozens of times, but the mere idea of overthrowing the government was more frightening than anything he'd ever experienced. Not only the boldness of it but also the chance of his going down in history as a traitor. Then there was the fact that he could easily end up getting shot or be sentenced to a lethal injection.

Well, that he could accept. He had made the decision to offer his life for his country back when he was only eighteen. Then, he figured he might die on some foreign battlefield and be called a hero. At the moment, it looked as though he might die right there at home and be labeled a traitor. That thought hurt more than anything else.

Things had to be done right. He and Corbin needed to get in charge and start a united front against the aliens. Once the people of Earth saw the threat, they'd rally behind them. If he died fighting the aliens, at least he'd die a hero.

But that wouldn't happen unless he could make a quick strike and take over all the key government buildings and announce his coup. How could he do that without ending up with a bullet in his brain?

Then it hit him. The Atlanteans, of course. They were getting the best training and the best equipment, and they were completely in his power. Those were the soldiers he needed to strike Washington. With enough Atlanteans, he could take and hold the capital until the other military leaders fell into line. General Corbin would help, and there were probably others he didn't know about, others concerned about what was going on in the skies but who kept quiet for fear of hurting their careers.

Timing would be everything. He had to wait until the alien invasion was imminent and obvious. When the Earth trembled in fear, when the politicians looked useless in the face of the biggest danger the planet had ever faced, that would be the time to strike. The people wouldn't look at him as a traitor, they'd look at him as a savior.

He hoped.

First things first, he needed to get rid of the opposition, and that meant finding out what that captured Atlantean knew.

He entered the Poseidon Project lab and found Dr. Jones and Bill Ziegler had made it there ahead of him. Ziegler was a hypnotist General Meade had stolen from the Italian Mafia to use for his own purposes. The guy was utterly without morals. He'd practiced medicine with a fake license, had done jobs for the Mafia so he could shower his mistress with diamonds and fur coats while his wife sat clueless in a modest suburban home, and currently he was working for the Poseidon Project because Meade had offered him more than the Mafia had, plus immunity from prosecution.

The two men flanked an operating table on which the Atlantean lay. The man was in his late twenties, with the typical features of his people. His chest and one arm were bandaged from where Meade's agents had shot him. His eyes were shut. Thick straps of woven steel secured his arms and legs.

"Is he conscious?" Meade asked as he went up to the operating table.

"Not yet," Dr. Jones said, picking up a hypodermic needle from a tray of medical equipment set on a table next to the patient. "I'll wake him up now."

"How is he?"

"Remarkably well. His bullet wounds look like they've been healing for weeks instead of days. I estimate he'll be perfectly fine within seventy-two hours."

General Meade shook his head in amazement. That fellow had taken a bullet through the right lung, and another bullet had severed the main artery in his left arm. Because of the fight and the need to hide him from the regular police and hospital staff, he hadn't received medical attention for almost an hour. Any normal human would have bled to death long before that.

Dr. Jones continued. "A couple of his team members weren't any worse off, and they died. Bled out before the paramedics got there. You know how I was saying each Atlantean has a special power? I think this man's power is rapid healing. Even though your average Atlantean is tough, they're nothing like this guy. They can still go down if hit by a bullet."

General Meade ground his teeth. That made it easier to fight the group, but it also meant that his own regiment of Atlanteans would be more vulnerable. He'd have to ask the Pentagon to assign him some more medics. Great, more paperwork.

"What's his name?"

Dr. Jones shook his head. "He didn't have any ID on him."

Dr. Jones gave the prisoner an injection. Ziegler leaned over the patient, dangling a shiny metal ball at the end of a string.

"As he wakes up, he'll be at his most impressionable," the hypnotist explained. "I will try to put him under the influence. If you could use the same drugs you used on Orion, that would help."

Dr. Joes shook his head. "Not in his condition."

The prisoner's eyes fluttered, shut again for a moment, and finally opened. Those brilliant blue eyes fixated on the shiny metal ball, which Ziegler started to swing on the end of the string like a pendulum.

"Relax," Ziegler said in soothing tones. "You're safe. You're in a hospital. You're safe. We're here to help. We've given you the best medical attention. You're going to be fine. Could you tell us your name, sir?"

General Meade nodded in appreciation. That "sir" on the end was a nice touch. Gave the Atlantean the impression that he was a patient, not a prisoner.

"Arturo Robles."

"Could you give us your address?" Ziegler asked, spinning the ball around on the end of the string so it caught the light. General Meade could see it flickering in the Atlantean's eyes.

"2323 East Cesar Chavez Boulevard," Robles said, naming a street in East LA.

"You have been in a car accident, Mr. Robles. Could you tell us who was in the vehicle with you?"

"A car accident? I—" Robles turned his head and tried to move his arm. The restraints let him move only an inch. He stared at his arm in confusion, trying to focus his vision.

"Mr. Robles," Ziegler said. "Look at me. That's it. I need to ask you some questions. Who was with you in the car? What are their names?"

Robles looked at him. For an instant, there was awareness.

"I—" Robles's voice trailed off. His eyes shut, and he let out a sigh.

Ziegler turned to Dr. Jones, who looked down at the patient thoughtfully.

"Bull," General Meade grumbled. He poked Robles in his good shoulder. "Stop faking."

Robles's eyes snapped open. They fixated on General Meade, glinting with hate.

"I want to see my lawyer," the Atlantean demanded.

General Meade gave a grim smile and shook his head. "There are no lawyers in this dark hole, Mr. Robles. I'd talk if I were you."

Robles turned his head and looked up at the ceiling.

"The others are dead?"

"Maybe."

"And Dr. Yamazaki?"

"We caught her. She's in a prison cell just down the hall from the one we've reserved for you."

Robles snorted. "Maybe."

General Meade gripped the Atlantean's jaw and yanked his head so he faced him. Dr. Jones let out a cry of disagreement that Meade ignored.

"Name the other people on your team," the general said.

"Go to hell," Robles said.

General Meade tightened his grip on the man's jaw as the scientist and the hypnotist looked on, their eyes wide. After a minute, he loosened his grip. "Never mind. We have your name and address. That's all we need to track them down. What I really want to know, and what I'll really hurt you to tell me, is how many Atlanteans are in your group."

Robles looked at him, confused. "Huh?"

"How many Atlanteans are in your group? Are there other groups like yours?" General Meade asked, growing uncertain.

"What the hell are you talking about?"

General Meade stared at him. No, the man wasn't shamming. Robles really didn't know what he was talking about.

Could it be that none of those people knew what they were? So far, he had found no evidence that they did, but he had assumed when he found an organized group that they'd have some sort of idea of where they had come from.

"Your people, what are they?" the general demanded.

Robles said nothing.

"Dr. Jones, give the injection."

"He's still very weak."

"That's an order."

The scientist hesitated for a moment and then picked up another hypo. It was a serum Meade had used in various theaters of war. It caused acute to excruciating pain without actually harming the individual. More refined and less barbaric than waterboarding or sleep deprivation or good old-fashioned punching. Meade had never enjoyed interrogation, but at times it was necessary.

Unfortunately for Arturo Robles, it was one of those times.

General Meade had to hand it to him, for someone who had taken two bullets only to wake up and find all his friends dead and himself officially missing, he had a lot of spirit left. As the injection kicked in and sweat beaded on the Atlantean's brow, as his muscles strained against his bonds, as his teeth ground and a scream came from his lips, he had nothing to say to his captors.

Dr. Jones gave him a second injection, doubling the pain. That didn't weaken Robles's determination.

He started talking, though. Said all sorts of creative things about Meade's personal life, his mother, and things he'd do to both if he ever got free. Meade learned a dozen new vocabulary words he'd never actually say. Then he started in on Jones and Ziegler.

The scientist looked pale and nervous, clearly uncomfortable with what he would call torture.

The hypnotist, on the other hand, didn't look bothered at all. He sat a little distance away, watching with interest. Meade figured he'd seen a lot worse during his time in the Mafia.

After the third injection, Arturo Robles started screaming and crying. He still didn't talk. His body bucked and writhed so much he tore one of his wounds open. Meade wanted to give him a fourth injection, but Dr. Jones put his foot down.

"His system can't take any more of this," Dr. Jones said. He'd also said it with the second and third injections, but that time, Meade believed him.

The general sighed. "Well, it's late. I guess we won't get anything out of him this time. Patch him up, put him in a cell, and we'll deal with him later."

Meade bent down and grabbed Robles's jaw again. It was slick with sweat. "And there will be a later, trust me. I'm going to make you talk if it's the last thing I do."

Robles's eyes widened in fear.

Meade stormed off. He exited the laboratory and headed for his office. His assistant, Major Jefferson, was there to meet him. She held a pair of dossiers.

"I've been going through the blacklist," Major Jefferson said.

General Meade turned to her, eager to hear what she had to say.

"I've eliminated most of the suspects and narrowed the list down to two," she said. "A few of your enemies were clearly not the culprits. You'll be happy to know that Albert Jennings turned up dead last month in Oklahoma. Someone shot him. Police have no suspects."

"Somebody beat me to it? Good," General Meade said. "That's one less headache. Try to find out who killed him and why."

"Will do. Intelligence reports show that several other people on the list were in other regions of the country at the time of the fight in New Mexico. No way they could have made it down there in time to be involved. A couple of others, Gloria Alberts and Maggie Dennison, are down in the Bahamas, supposedly on vacation."

"A sniper and an explosives expert getting a tan in the Caribbean? I find that hard to believe."

"So do I. There have been a couple of killings down there since they showed up. I'm checking on that."

The general nodded in appreciation. While there was a time when he had resisted the inclusion of women in the military, and he still thought it was wrong to let them on combat missions, he had to concede that some female officers had proven to be indispensable. Major Jefferson was one of them. She had a tenacity and an attention to detail that most male officers lacked. Women made good independent operatives too, as Ms. Alberts and Ms. Dennison had proven time and time again. Not to mention Isadore Grant. She was the most dangerous woman he had ever met.

"So who does that leave?" General Meade asked.

"Only two people," Major Jefferson said. "Two of the worst. Vivian Gulland and Philip Sellmeyer, who's going by the nickname 'Grunt.'"

The major handed over the dossiers. General Meade didn't have to look at them. He knew their histories well enough.

With those two up against him, he needed to get his agents in order. He needed to eliminate those two right away, or they'd eliminate him.

It wouldn't be the first time they had killed a general.

Chapter 16

JUNE 30, 2016, COUNTY HIGHWAY
NEAR APACHE JUNCTION, ARIZONA

1:05 AM

Otto and Grunt drove through the first half of the night, passing along remote county roads as usual. Grunt had returned to his normal joking self, although Otto could sense an underlying tension.

He guessed that Grunt was trying to make up for snapping at him, and that was the closest thing to an apology he could manage. Otto tried not to take it personally. He didn't know what was going through the mercenary's mind, after all. Otto had spent his whole life being judged by people who didn't know him, and he wasn't about to do the same with Grunt.

At one point, Grunt asked Otto to stop the Hummer so they could change the license plates. Grunt had a whole collection of plates from different states in a secret compartment in the back. Most of the Tohono O'odham pickup trucks went on the interstate since their drivers had clean records. Jim Running Horse drove his pickup a mile behind the Hummer. He changed his plates too.

About one in the morning, Grunt told him to pull off at a rest stop, a quiet place in the desert with nothing but a restroom, and closed. The other vehicles were already there, except for the trailers that carried the rest of the Atlantis Allegiance.

"Since they're driving slow in the trailers, they're going on ahead," Grunt said.

"And what are we going to do?" Otto asked as he turned off the lights. He didn't need to be told something was up. He could tell by the fact that while all the pickups were parked nearby, not a single Tohono O'odham was in sight.

"We're going to do something entirely optional," Grunt replied. "But come take a look and decide for yourself if you want to be a part of it or not."

They got out of the Hummer and walked to the edge of the parking lot. A low whistle out in the darkness made them turn and step into the desert. Another low whistle led them on. Their feet crunched on rocky soil. The stars shone brightly overhead, and the moon rose to the east, giving them light enough to avoid the cacti. After about thirty feet, Jim Running Horse and a couple of his friends emerged from the shadows.

"We've been listening to police chatter on the scanner," one of the men said. With a jolt, Otto realized that was the guy he had stolen the lighter from. "There won't be a patrol car passing by for at least twenty-five minutes."

"Time enough," Grunt said.

Jim Running Horse led the way. Otto peered into the darkness, trying to pick a safe path through a thick growth of cacti and agave. The Tohono O'odham passed through it without slowing down. Grunt hissed as a thorn jabbed his calf. Otto smiled. It was nice to see the guy wasn't invulnerable. They came to a chain-link fence topped with barbed wire. A section of the fence had been cut open wide enough to slip through. Otto spotted a small sign and the emblem of a major security company.

"You guys sure you didn't trip the alarm?" Otto asked.

"We tripped it when we cut open the fence," Jim Running Horse said.

"Come on," Otto grumbled. Why didn't those people take him seriously?

"I mean it," he insisted, his grin bright in the moonlight.

"Did Edward hack into the security company site or something?" Otto asked.

"You're learning, Pyro." Grunt chuckled. "Those security boys back at their headquarters are reading all clear for this place."

On the other side of the fence, they met up with the rest of the Tohono O'odham. They all wore dark clothing, and several of them carried bolt cutters and other tools.

The group walked for another ten feet or so and came to an area of churned-up earth. All the cacti, bushes, and big rocks had been cleared away. Instead of the subtle scents of the desert, Otto smelled gasoline and freshly turned soil. Not far off loomed the silhouettes of several tractors.

"What is this?" he asked.

Jim Running Horse turned to him. "This is a burial ground for the Hohokam. They were ancestors to my people and lived here about a thousand years ago."

"Yeah, but what about all this construction?"

"Test mine for uranium. Big money in nuclear power," he replied, his voice laced with bitterness.

"But...it's right next to a rest stop!"

"So what? It's on private land."

"But if they find uranium, the rest stop will get hit by radiation, won't it?"

Jim Running Horse shrugged. "Just a little. Might give some people cancer in twenty, thirty years. The feds look the other way. Besides, it's on private land like I told you. What gets carried in the air isn't really their business, is it?"

"So it's not illegal to do this?"

"Not in any serious way," Grunt said. "They don't care about the living or the dead."

The group spread out. Some went to the bulldozers, while others scattered across the site.

"What are you going to do?" Otto asked, tagging alongside the Tohono O'odham leader.

"We're going to pull up all the survey stakes and wreck their equipment."

"But that's illegal!"

"Under your law it's illegal. Under my law it's illegal to desecrate a burial ground."

Otto stared for a moment, stunned, then said, "But it's not like you're going to stop them by doing that. They'll just add some more security to the site, bring in more bulldozers, and keep working."

Jim Running Horse shook his head. "No, we won't stop them the first time, but if we keep hitting them, they might just decide it's not so profitable to work here, and they'll go off to dig someplace else."

He turned and walked off into the night.

Grunt pulled something out of a small backpack he carried. He held it up so Otto could see. It was a packet of bulk food like ones sold in the supermarket.

"Care to join me?" he asked, then turned and walked away before Otto could reply.

Otto followed, his heart pounding. What did that have to do with their mission?

Grunt hurried over to a pair of bull-dozers parked side by side. One of the Tohono O'odham had opened the hood and was busy clipping cables in the engine. Grunt went up to the other bulldozer, unscrewed the cap to the gas tank, and poured something from the packet into the tank.

"What's that?" Otto asked.

"Sugar," Grunt replied, carefully watching as it poured into the tank. "If they're dumb enough to turn on the engine, it will get flooded with sugar mixed with gas. That will wreck an engine worse than emptying my nine millimeter into it."

Grunt then took out his canteen and poured some water into the tank.

"Water is heavier than gasoline, so it will settle on the bottom of the tank along with the sugar," he explained. "When they turn on the ignition, the water will flood the engine, seizing it up, and the sugar will grind down everything."

Otto gave the nearby road a nervous glance.

"How is this helping Jaxon? We're taking a risk for no reason."

"Keep your voice down, Pyro. There are plenty of fights enough in the world for everybody. The T.O. have helped us out, so we help them out. You don't freeload off your allies, kid."

"This is illegal," Otto repeated. He wasn't sure what else to say.

"Says the pyromaniac who broke out of prison and threw grenades at government agents."

"That was different. They were trying to kill us."

Otto realized that only justified half the stuff he had done. For once, Grunt was polite enough not to point that out.

"They're trying to kill the Native Americans too. Erase their history, desecrate their holy places, make them look like savages in the movies. Killing their spirit works just as well as killing their bodies."

Grunt had moved on to another tractor and started pouring sugar into the tank.

"Are you part Native American?" Otto asked.

Grunt shook his head. His features were hidden in the dim light, and Otto wondered what his expression was. "Don't need to be. Jim has been my friend for years, and some of the others have done me a good turn too. In the end, we're all on the same side."

Grunt finished his work and handed him the half-empty sugar packet. Suddenly he grabbed Otto and pushed him down to the ground. Grunt lay right next to him. The Tohono O'odham got down too.

A distant set of headlights appeared on the highway. Otto could hear his heart thumping against the loose soil. Had the patrol car shown up early?

The car whooshed by them without slowing down. Otto let out the breath he had been holding. He and Grunt got back on their feet.

"Why don't you take that backhoe over there?" the mercenary said. "You've seen how it's done."

Otto looked at the packet in his hand. "But the mining company isn't our enemy," he objected.

"Yeah it is, I just explained it to you."

Otto paused. That went against everything he had been taught, and yet what Grunt and the Tohono O'odham said made sense in a way. After a moment, he shook his head.

"No. This isn't what I signed up for."

"Want to burn it instead?"

Otto's eyes widened, and his heart did a flip-flop. He felt a warm flush over his body. The stolen lighter in his pocket called to him.

"You sure?" Otto asked. He heard his words come out in a harsh whisper.

Grunt chuckled. "Just kidding. The fire would get spotted from the road." Grunt took the packet from him and used the other hand to playfully slap Otto on the cheek a few times. "You need to get your priorities straight, kid."

Otto hung his head. That had been a test, and he'd failed. Resentment simmered up in him. Who was that guy to lecture him? He was running around there destroying private property instead of keeping on with the mission, and he had already said he wasn't going to see it through to the end. Grunt might have been able to snap him in half, but Otto had more guts than he did. Otto thought of a few snappy answers to show the mercenary just where they stood, but he couldn't bring himself to say them. Maybe he didn't have the guts after all.

The others began to gather near the fence. Otto went over to them.

"Edward says we got ten minutes to get out of here before a patrol car comes into view," Jim Running Horse said. Otto could barely make out an earpiece running from the man's phone to his ear.

The Tohono O'odham began to clear out. Grunt came hurrying up.

"All set," he said.

"Did he help?" Jim Running Horse asked, pointing his chin in Otto's direction. It was a strange habit the Tohono O'odham had. They never pointed at anything with their finger.

"It's illegal," Grunt said in a little-girl voice.

Jim Running Horse scoffed. "You got to school this youngster, my friend, or he's going to get you killed one day."

Early the next morning, Otto drove the Hummer along a lonely stretch of highway as Grunt sat in the passenger's seat. They had rejoined the trailers but kept their distance so no one would notice they were together. The trailer Vivian was driving was a quarter of a mile ahead of them, and they saw her pull into a convenience store and gas station.

"Let's get some coffee," Grunt said.

"Fine by me," Otto replied, pulling off the highway.

It was early in the morning, and Otto's eyes were gritty and red from another night of trying to sleep in the backseat of a car. He really wished the Atlantis Allegiance would put up at a motel every once in a while, but that would be too risky. Grunt had been quiet for much of the night, but he had started making casual conversation with Otto as the sun rose. It seemed as though he was trying to make amends for the previous night's outburst. Otto still didn't know what it was all about. Perhaps he'd learn in time.

As Vivian filled the gas tank to the trailer, they walked into the store, pretending they didn't know her. The bright fluorescent lights stung Otto's eyes. The place had the usual aisles full of junk food plus a little diner attached with a few tables and a row of stools at a counter. The only people inside at that hour were a bored-looking teenager at the register and a businessman sipping a coffee and reading a newspaper at the counter.

"Two jumbo coffees, black," Grunt told the teenager.

"I take cream and sugar in mine," Otto said.

"Wimp. There's no caffeine in cream and sugar," Grunt said. He turned to the guy at the register. "He'll have his black."

Otto shrugged. Looked as though Grunt was back to his old self again. As the attendant poured the coffee into two giant Styrofoam cups, they went over to the refrigerator and grabbed some sodas and energy drinks for later.

"We got a long day ahead." Otto sighed.

"Don't worry. We'll get a good night's sleep tonight. Best to be fresh before getting down to business."

Otto tensed. More wasted time. They should save Jaxon as soon as they got to Los Angeles. On second thought, though, it made sense to get rested. When they went in to get her, they'd have to deal with two of General Meade's best agents and who knew what else. Then they'd probably get chased and be on the run for a while. No telling how long it would be before they could rest easy.

So yeah, Jaxon would have to hold tight for another day. Edward said she was in no immediate danger.

Otto grabbed a few donuts, and he and Grunt went to the counter and paid for the food. They didn't pay for Vivian's gas. As she came in, they continued to ignore her, and she ignored them.

"Come on, Pyro. Time to get going," Grunt said.

As they headed out the door, Vivian ordered two coffees and a pair of Danishes and paid for the gas.

Otto saw the businessman glance over his newspaper at her and then go back to reading. Vivian appeared not to have noticed. Men looked at her all the time.

***

As Vivian left the store, the businessman lowered his newspaper just enough to see the two men get into the Hummer and the woman get into the trailer home. He noticed a Japanese woman sitting in the passenger's seat of the trailer. He watched as the Hummer and the trailer home pulled away. Once both vehicles were out of sight, he pulled his cell phone out of his pocket and made a call.

Chapter 17

AUGUST 2, 2016, ALBUQUERQUE,
NEW MEXICO

9:00 AM

General Meade walked down the line of his agents as they stood at attention. A dozen of them stood there, dressed in identical black suits with identical black sunglasses tucked in their front pockets because they stood in the Poseidon Project's indoor training room.

The general noted they all kept perfect attention. All were in excellent shape, all trained to fight, all ex-military.

But he noted something else too. The youngest was in his mid-thirties. Some were in their forties. None of them had seen a combat operation in years. They were all ex-soldiers signed up for Army Intelligence because they couldn't adjust to civilian life. An agent's pay was much better than that of some soldier in a war zone, the benefits were excellent, and much of the duty was comparatively light.

That was the problem. Those guys were accustomed to tapping the phones of suspected terrorists or tracking down illegal arms dealers, not fighting Atlanteans with superior abilities and special powers. They couldn't even handle Dr. Yamazaki. They made a big show of bringing her in at the start of everything, making everyone at her university start whispering rumors and conspiracy theories, and then she got away from the hospital. Those idiots were out of their league.

So it was time to up their game.

"Gentlemen, you have a new unit commander. Orion, come over here."

Orion stepped up beside his master. General Meade noticed the agents' eyes go wide as they recognized Orion for what he was.

"That's right, men. Orion here is an Atlantean. And you'll soon be joined by more of them. If you're going to defeat the Atlantean terrorist group that's threatening national security, you're going to have to use Atlanteans against them, just like we use patriotic Muslims to infiltrate Islamist groups. You'll be training with Orion on a specially prepared field we have here on base. And you'll be getting better weapons, assault rifles and grenades. You'll get body armor too. You're going up against the best, so you'll be given the best gear and the best training. It's going to be hard. Are you ready for it?"

"Sir, yes, sir!" they shouted in unison.

"You're going to become the baddest killers in the country, aren't you?"

"Sir, yes, sir!" they shouted again.

"Now go, go, GO!" General Meade shouted, clapping his hands. Orion ran out of the room and headed for the door. The agents fell in line behind him. Meade followed and watched as Orion led them out onto the training ground.

Suddenly, soldiers in camouflage popped up from half a dozen hiding places and pelted them with paint pellets. Orion ducked and rolled. He was the only one not to get hit. The agents stood there, confused, their suits covered in red paint.

General Meade nodded with approval. Let them train with real soldiers for a change, and let them get those damn suits dirty for once.

The soldiers dropped their weapons and charged. That was another special surprise Meade had planned for the idiots. They leaped onto the agents, their fists flying, their booted feet kicking. The agents rallied and started fighting back. Even though the soldiers were ten, fifteen years younger, they found themselves fighting their match as experience dueled with youth.

Soon the whole thing degenerated into a brawl. The agents, their precious egos hurt, showed the soldiers no mercy. The soldiers, for their part, weren't about to let a bunch of old farts defeat them. An agent staggered back, blood spurting from his broken nose. A soldier got flipped head over heels and cracked his head on the ground, knocking him unconscious. Orion stood a little apart from the fight, laughing at both sides.

Meade laughed too. That was just what the men needed. The army was stretched too thin overseas to pull anyone out of a combat zone, so he had to create one. The rivalry between the younger troops and the older agents would help beat both sides into shape, and if a few people got hurt, well, that was just how the world was.

His phone rang. When he answered, Isadore Grant's voice came over the line.

"So how is Jaxon doing?" Meade asked.

"There's been an unusual development. Jaxon has taken to sneaking out at night. Stephen and I have been taking turns following her. At first we worried that she was sneaking out to see a boy. It wouldn't do to have your future soldier become pregnant. But it turns out she's doing something more interesting. She's become a vigilante."

"A vigilante?"

"She got the idea from a local vigilante who has been appearing in the LA news. She wrote a school paper about it and started sneaking out soon afterward, looking for trouble. Of course a young girl alone at night in LA will find plenty of it."

"She hasn't been hurt, has she?" General Meade asked.

"No, she's been able to handle everything the city has thrown at her, and she's hooked up with the other vigilante too, the one who originally inspired her."

General Meade was about to ask a question when Isadore predicted it.

"No, he's not an Atlantean, just a normal teenage boy. Turns out he's from Jaxon's school. We tried to find out if there was something behind all this, but it looks like it's just a coincidence. The boy knows a bit of martial arts and has some street smarts. It won't last, though. The kid is bound to get hurt sooner or later."

"And Jaxon?"

"She'll be fine as long as she doesn't come up against a gang or someone with some decent firepower. I'm thinking this is good field training for her."

"You're right, it is, but our schedule has to be sped up. We need to make her training a bit more rigorous."

"You want us to create an incident?"

"Just steer her in the wrong direction, and she'll create her own."

"What if she gets injured? Or killed?"

"She'll heal from her injuries soon enough," General Meade said. "And if she gets killed, well, that's just a risk we'll have to take."

"Sounds good to me," Isadore said. "Stephen had already suggested something along those lines."

General Meade smiled. Yes, he had been right to entrust the mission to those two. Cold-blooded, the both of them.

"I have an idea that will test her abilities to the utmost," Isadore said. "It will either make her or break her."

General Meade watched as the agents and soldiers kept battering at each other, their clothing torn and their features bloody.

"Do whatever you think is best," he said. "And if she breaks, well, too damn bad."

About the Author

S.A. Beck lives in sunny California. When she's not surfing, knitting or daydreaming in a hammock, she's writing novels.

S.A. Beck

www.ingramcontent.com/pod-product-compliance
Lightning Source LLC
Chambersburg PA
CBHW052022240626
47153CB00006B/1912